THE ARCANES OF THE BLACK ROSE

Chronicles of Elysorium - Volume 1

Olivier Elophe

I would like to express my gratitude to Mnemosyne, goddess of memory and mother of the Muses, for the constant inspiration she has bestowed upon me throughout the creation of this book.

I would also like to extend my heartfelt thanks to Sophie, my proofreader for the English version, for her patience and her knowledge of ancient magic, both of which have been invaluable to this journey.

CONTENTS

Title Page

Dedication

Introduction

Explore ELysorium

Chapter 1: The Rose's Choice — 1

Chapter 2: The Lily and the Rose — 18

Chapter 3: The Darkness of Elysorium — 33

Chapter 4: The Arcane Pearl — 41

Chapter 5: An Important Mission — 53

Chapter 6: The Challenge — 76

Chapter 7: Crossed Destinies — 89

Chapter 8: The Golden Fury — 97

Chapter 9: The City of Mages — 109

Chapter 10: The City of the Sun — 120

Chapter 11: The Angel and the Colossus — 138

Chapter 12: The Grasp of the Abyss — 152

Chapter 13: Confrontation	170
Chapter 14: Epilogue	182
The Chronicles of Elysorium	193

INTRODUCTION

Welcome to the first volume of the Elysorium chronicles, a world sculpted by magic and myth, where destinies intertwine in the grand weaving of time. This is but the start of a journey that will carry you through lands as diverse as they are enthralling, from the impenetrable jungles of Stellarae in the south to the snow-capped peaks of Frostend in the north, from the lush capital of Valoria to the sun-drenched city-states of Maridora.

Each character you meet has their own story, hidden secrets, and deep aspirations. From mages whose immense powers weave the fabric of intrigues to warriors whose legendary strength shapes history with their swords, the range of souls you will encounter is vast and varied. Paladins, epic figures of virtue, stand as bastions against the forces of darkness, while assassins, masters of shadow, act where light fades. Beyond these well-trodden paths, discover a multitude of other character classes, each with unique skills and roles to play in the vast theater of Elysorium.

Here, the echoes of ancient magic resonate in deep valleys, and forgotten ruins await those daring enough to uncover their secrets. The seas and mountains of Elysorium are more than mere geographic expanses; they are the beating heart of a living world, home to peoples and creatures whose stories intersect under the gaze of the gods themselves.

Your immersion into the Elysorium chronicles is an epic where each revelation blossoms into enigma, where every unlocked key reveals hidden doors. Let yourself be guided by the whispers of the Icarion Sea and root yourself in the eternal erudition of Seranthea. Each chapter unveils a new horizon, an invitation to wonder and contemplation.

In this tale, solving one mystery is only the birth of another, each uncovered truth weaving the beginnings of a deeper secret. The adventure unfolding before you is a complex tapestry where the light of each solved enigma only casts new shadows on mysteries yet to be touched.

Embark on this epic saga where the resolution of each plot is the prelude to a greater mystery. Here, at the heart of the world of Elysorium, every end is a new beginning, every conclusion opens the path to unexplored legends. May your journey be filled with exhilarating revelations and captivating mysteries, for here, every tale shapes the dawn of new, magnificent adventures.

EXPLORE ELYSORIUM

✻ ✻ ✻

For an even deeper immersion into the world of 'The Chronicles of Elysorium', scan the QR code below to discover the map of Elysorium. Travel through the known and mysterious lands our heroes traverse in their epic adventures.

CHAPTER 1: THE ROSE'S CHOICE

Prologue: Valoria

Perched like a crown at the heart of Elysorium's Fertile Lands, Valoria stands, a majestic capital where poets' dreams and kings' ambitions come to life. It's a crossroads of civilization, an eagle's nest from which one's gaze embraces the entirety of the Elysorium kingdom. Dominating the Thorneira region, bordered by the gentle whispers of the Verdania Forest to the west and the peaceful waves of the Bay of Angels to the east, Valoria is the glittering jewel of this world, the synthesis of a rich history and an even greater destiny.

Approaching the city, the traveler is first welcomed by the Verdant Fields of Valoria, expanses of farmland that wrap the city like a greenish mantle, dotted with golden patches where wheat and barley sway under the caress of the wind. Here is where the beating heart of the city draws its life, nourished by the harvests and the winding rivers that meander through the meadows.

The walls of Valoria, built by the ancients and fortified by time, rise like stone giants, silent witnesses of the centuries past. They tell stories of sieges, triumphs, and heartbreaks, while tirelessly guarding the treasures they enclose. The main entrance, the Dawn Gate, opens like an invitation, its panels engraved with tales of dragons and deities, reflecting the splendor and power of Valoria.

Inside its walls, the city is a living labyrinth, a kaleidoscope of activity where every paved alley, every square and market buzzes with the life of the Valorians. The markets of Valoria are colorful chaos, where the spices of Maridora mingle with the fabrics of Silvaria and the rare metals of Frostend. The cries of the merchants, the bursts of laughter, and the sounds of bartering contribute to the city's daily symphony.

The Central Square, the beating heart of Valoria, is a spectacle in itself. It's there that the famous debates are held, where the scholars and philosophers from Seranthea and Stellarae argue over the nature of reality and the stars. The fountains, sculpted in the image of the Elysorium goddesses, pour out crystal-clear water, offering a soothing melody that contrasts with the surrounding bustle.

At the center of Valoria rises the Upper City, a collection of palaces and hanging gardens where the nobility resides. There, the watchtowers and palaces with roofs of gold and slate sparkle under the sun, an enchanting sight for any newcomer.

At night, the city transforms into a terrestrial constellation, lit by thousands of lanterns and torches that outline a dreamlike world.

And above all, towers the Queen's Palace, an architectural masterpiece that seems to touch the sky itself. With its slender spires and opulent domes, it is the symbol of Valoria's grandeur, a place where decisions shaping the fate of Elysorium are made.

But Valoria is not only about splendor and light. As the brilliance of the upper city twinkled under the firmament, bathed in the golden light of its towers and palaces, the docks and lower quarters of the city presented a striking contrast, a tangle of shadows and mysteries where each alley told a darker story.

In the lower depths, the buildings crowded against each other, forming a labyrinth of narrow, twisting streets. The worn pavements were imbued with the footsteps of thousands of lives, of intertwined destinies. Here, far from the crystalline splendor of the upper echelons, mingled the voices of the marginalized, the refugees, the non-humans struggling to find their place in a world that offered them little mercy.

The docks, battered by sea winds, buzzed with the incessant activity of merchants, sailors, and smugglers. Robust dwarves unloaded cargoes, their bulging muscles a testament to a strength forged in the bowels of the earth. Elves, with slender ears and eyes filled with millennial wisdom, strolled with an almost unreal grace, their whispers lost in the surrounding din.

Taverns, scattered like dark pearls in the necklace of alleys, teemed with life. Their signs creaked in the wind, inviting weary souls to take refuge in the warmth of their smoky insides. Inside, laughter mingled with verbal jousting, songs rose above the clinking of mugs, and stories intertwined like the threads of a complex fabric.

In the dark corners, shielded from view, dubious items were traded: fake phoenix feathers shining with deceptive brilliance, alleged griffin blood sold under the counter, and a thousand other counterfeit wonders designed to deceive the untrained eye. These illusory treasures changed hands with the speed of a blink, the whispered exchanges melting into the air laden with untold stories.

But despite its roughness, this underground world possessed a raw beauty, a dark luster shining with a light different from that of the upper city. It was a place where survival brushed against dreams, where each smile hid a story, and every gaze reflected a burning desire to live fully, despite the trials.

In these less luminous quarters of the jewel that was the city, life flowed with a feverish intensity, a mix of despair and hope, danger and promise. It was a place where anything was possible, where each encounter could change a life, and where each step could lead either to a dizzying fall or to an unexpected ascent.

And so, in the shadow of the magnificent towers of the city, beat the true heart of the city, a heart animated by the indomitable strength of those who walked in the darkness, their eyes fixed on the stars hidden behind the veils of the night.

Valoria is thus this living mosaic, a microcosm of Elysorium in all its glory and complexity. It's a city where every dream can flourish, where every hope can take root, and where the threads of destiny are as diverse as the stars in Elysorium's endless nocturnal sky.

❋ ❋ ❋

The Thorns Of The Rose

In the depths of the night enveloping Valoria, where only the pale glow of swaying lanterns pierce the darkness, the whispers of an eternally awake city float in the air. On the worn cobblestones of the capital, shadows dance, weaving ancient and new stories. Among them moves a figure, as silent as a buried secret, as deadly as a whisper of forgotten truth.

Iris Blackthorn, the Black Rose, advances with discreet assurance, the hood of her cloak casting a veil over a face marked by determination and the secrets she carries. In her gloved hand, a single ebony rose, as dark as the mission entrusted to her. This rose is an omen, a harbinger of death for those who receive it, and tonight, it must find its place under the door of a wealthy abode, that of a priestess whose fate has been sealed by powers that play with life and death.

Valoria, a labyrinth of light and shadow, seems to hold its breath as Iris traverses the noble quarter, a place where wealth and power barely mask the corruption and conspiracies fermenting beneath their opulent facades. She knows these streets like the lines of her hand, every nook, every hiding spot, every whisper carried by the wind.

The path to the priestess's abode is fraught with dangers, for the night belongs as much to thieves and bandits as to the shadow creatures that thrive in the darkness. But Iris fears neither men nor monsters; she is a far greater danger, a force that even the darkness respects.

Having arrived at her destination, she slips like a

shadow among shadows, her sharp gaze scanning the surroundings before placing the black rose - her signature, her warning - under the solid wood door. It's a signal that the priestess will only see when it's too late, a final gift from a life soon to be cut short.

With her act completed, Iris retreats into the darkness, patient and still. She waits for the right moment to enter and finish her mission. But tonight, fate has woven a different pattern, and what was meant to be an act of death could well turn into a path towards the truth.

In the lair of the night, the Black Rose begins to doubt, for every flower, even the darkest, aspires to the light...

This whisper of ancient wisdom, like a distant echo, insinuated itself into the mind of Iris Blackthorn as she melted back into the shadow. It was a lesson from her early days in the sect of the Black Roses, a maxim repeated with the rigor of the blades she was learning to wield. "Even in the deepest darkness, Iris, a rose must seek the light," Master Kali would teach her, his voice as sharp as his eyes were gentle. "It is in this quest that your strength lies, not in the embrace of the shadow."

She remembered the training room, the walls draped with dried black roses, their thorns as sharp as the daggers placed in her hands. "Light is not just what reveals you, child," Kali would say as he guided her through the movements of the shadow, "it's what defines you." Iris learned to dance with darkness, to move in silence, but also to understand that every act of darkness had to be counterbalanced by a thread of light, however thin it might be.

She was taught to kill, yes, but she was also taught the weight of life. "Every breath you extinguish is an echo in eternity," whispered the priestess of the sect, her hands as cold as death placed on Iris's shoulders. "Never take death lightly, for each life is a thread in the tapestry of the world. Breaking a thread can unravel nations, weaving a new one can build dynasties."

These lessons shaped Iris, forging her into a weapon, but they also gave her a perspective few assassins possessed. In each target, she saw not just a mission, but a question, a reflection on the role she played in the grand scheme of fate.

❉ ❉ ❉

The Roots Of The Rose

As the moon reaches its zenith, casting a silvery light over the rooftops of Valoria, Iris approaches the abode of the priestess, ready to execute the contract that binds her life to the death of another. Against all odds, the door opens before she touches the handle. Standing before her is the priestess, of serene beauty, with eyes shining with a light that seems to defy the fatality of the situation.

"I know who you are, Black Rose," says the priestess with a voice tinged with resigned melancholy. "I understand the meaning of the flower you placed at my threshold. But do you truly understand who you are? Do you know what happened to your mother, the real reason why you were chosen by the sect?"

Iris, usually the shadow that surprises, finds herself disconcerted. She conceals her turmoil, but her mind is in turmoil. How can this priestess know these details of her life, even unknown to herself? Instinct screams at her to flee, but curiosity and an unexplored desire for truth hold her back.

Iris, her eyes filled with a cold intensity, addressed the priestess with a cutting voice: "Speak, priestess. Choose carefully the words that might be your last."

The priestess, with a steadfast gaze and a voice laden with seriousness, replied, "Listen attentively to the secrets I am about to reveal about your past. Then, in your soul and conscience, decide who deserves to live... and who must be condemned to death."

"I knew your mother, Iris," the priestess began, her eyes probing the assassin's soul with a disturbing intensity. "She was a heroine in the truest terms, a fearless guardian determined to thwart the return of the Black Dragon, that beast of ancient legends threatening to consume our world in ashes."

The priestess paused, allowing her words to seep into Iris's mind. "Your mother, an exceptional light mage, had dedicated her life to combating the forces of darkness. She knew that the Black Dragon was not just a story to scare children; it was a reality, an ancient and malevolent entity, chained by a powerful spell in the depths of a Land of Fire somewhere in Elysorium."

"She had discovered a prophecy," she continued, "a prediction that the Dragon would be freed by the hand of a necromancer blinded by power. She fought fervently to prevent this dark era from coming to pass, to keep the entity away from those who wished to exploit its devastating power."

Iris listened, each word awakening distant memories, images of a mother she had never truly known. "But her struggle put her in danger, Iris. She became the target of those who thirsted for power, including within our own city. She was betrayed by those she trusted, those who saw in her and her knowledge a threat to their ambitions."

"Your mother disappeared before you were entrusted to the sect of the Black Roses. Her disappearance was not an accident. It was a murder disguised as a common criminal act, designed to sow chaos and to hide the truth. She wanted you to be protected from these machinations, to live away from danger. But even in her final moments, she fought to ensure that the truth did not perish with her."

Iris's heart pounded furiously, a storm of rage and sorrow raging within her. "And now, Iris, you stand at a crossroads. You can choose to follow in your mother's footsteps, to fight for the light in a world shrouded in shadow, or you can continue on the path laid out for you, a path stained with the blood of the innocent."

The priestess stepped closer, placing a hand on Iris's shoulder. "The sect of the Black Roses trained you to be their weapon, but your mother's blood flows in your veins. It is up to you to decide whether you will be an instrument of death or the bearer of a new dawn for Elysorium."

Iris listens, each word revealing the lies that had been her only comfort. The priestess details the tortures endured by her mother, used by the necromancer and his ally, the Black General, to fuel their dark designs.

The priestess offers Iris a choice: remain the instrument of those who destroyed her family, or seek the truth and, perhaps, find redemption and vengeance. She advises Iris to head to the domain of the mages, where answers await her.

And now, faced with the priestess's revelations, these reflections deepen, pushing her towards a terrifying but necessary unknown.

Iris, with suspicion in her eyes, grasped her black blade, glistening with the deadly venom of desert scorpions. "You lie," she said with a voice laden with suspicion. Yet, in her training as a master assassin, she had developed the ability to detect lies in others, deep down she knew the truth was there, clear and undeniable, but it was as if her mind refused to accept it, a final spasm of denial in the face of a reality too painful to admit.

The priestess, panic piercing her voice, exclaimed hastily: "Wait... Find Archmage Valerius in Seranthea. He knew your mother. He knows everything. He knows where your sister is hiding."

At these words, Iris felt a dizziness seize her, as if long-buried memories were surging to the surface. "My sister..." This revelation shook something within her, as if the mention of her sister had cracked the mental armor forged by the Black Roses.

She left the room staggering, stunned by this revelation. It was as if the mere thought of her sister had chipped away at the solid wall built in her mind. Lost in a whirlwind of thoughts and emotions, Iris felt overwhelmed, confronted with a truth she wasn't sure she could face.

As she stood there, in the contemplative silence of the night, the priestess's words echoed with the teachings of Kali, her master.

The shattering revelations poured into her like a summer storm, unpredictable and liberating. The world she had known, a fabric of certainties woven in shadows, was now tearing apart, revealing an unsettling horizon of possibilities. The Black Rose, the symbol of her allegiance and her past, wilted in her hand, while a new determination took root.

The decision was made. It was time to leave the Black Roses, to turn her back on the order that had shaped her life, for the ties that held her were now as ephemeral as the morning mist. The quest for truth called to her, a call as irresistible as a siren's song to sailors lost at sea. She had to leave immediately and without looking back, for failing to complete her mission put her in danger – the Black Roses did not tolerate failure, and even less so, betrayal.

With the moon as her sole witness, Iris set off southward, towards Seranthea in Etheal, where the mages held the knowledge that would enable her to unravel the skein of her existence. The journey would be long, perhaps a full moon cycle if she hastened her pace, or two if fate decided to throw obstacles in her path. She would cross verdant valleys and mountain passes, scattered villages where travelers' tales intersect and are lost.

The night enveloped Iris in its cloak of darkness, transforming her into a shadow silently moving through Valoria. As she moved away from the place of her encounter with the priestess, each step she took was an act of rebellion against the darkness she had once embraced. Her gait was that of a predator, but her heart beat to the rhythm of a warrior in search of redemption.

Before leaving the city, Iris made a detour to her secret hideout, a lair known only to her, hidden in the forgotten interstices of Valoria. Here, she quickly gathered what she needed for her journey - some rations, a water flask, bandages, and of course, her faithful weapons. Each item was chosen for its functionality and minimal weight. She knew that speed and agility would be her allies in the quest that awaited her.

As she left the city through the south gate, the morning merchants were already setting up their stalls, a mosaic of colors and sounds awakening under the first rays of the sun. Iris crossed this living tableau, a solitary figure standing out against the backdrop of the morning bustle.

The stars, which had been her silent companions through the night, began to pale in the face of dawn's assault. They seemed to trace a celestial path, a luminous map towards a future filled with promises and mysteries.

As she moved away, the first light of dawn painted the sky in soft blue, heralding the end of an era of shadows and secrets. The forests of Thorneira, stretching out on the horizon, slowly awakened; the birds' songs welcomed the new day, oblivious to the turmoil of a soul in search of truth and freedom.

On her, Iris carried only the essentials, refusing to be weighed down by unnecessary burdens. She didn't look back, aware that every lost moment could mean her undoing. She moved forward, alone, but with the conviction that on the road to Seranthea, fate would reserve new encounters - potential allies, adversaries, trials, and triumphs. It was the beginning of a new chapter, the flight of a soul towards its destiny, as uncertain and magnificent as the dawn rising before her.

She knew the road to Etheal would be fraught with perils, but also discoveries. She would encounter learned mages, keepers of ancient secrets, and creatures born of pure magic. Iris was ready to learn, to fight, and to grow. She was ready to transform.

The Black Rose had left Valoria, but the one who now walked the winding path was no longer the same. She had become Iris Blackthorn, daughter of a light mage, warrior of a forgotten prophecy, the assassin who sought her path between light and darkness. The rising sun cast a golden light upon her, revealing the vast world of Elysorium that stretched out before her, rich in mysteries and promises.

But as she approached the Bridge of Legends, Iris sensed it was time to confront the one who had been following her since she left the city. An assassin like her could not be trailed so easily. With a determined step, she headed towards a place where she could face her pursuer, her assassin's instinct sharpened by the shadows of the past and the threat of the unknown.

CHAPTER 2: THE LILY AND THE ROSE

The Encounter

As the dawn light of Valoria bathed the city's cobblestones in a gentle amethyst glow, heralding a new day, Diane, the valiant-hearted heiress, felt the dawn bring with it the burden of an urgent quest and the thrill of clandestine adventure.

With her hood pulled over her golden hair, she blended into the crowd, a whisper among the murmurs of the breaking day. Her beauty, even veiled, was a beacon in the mist, drawing eyes as the moon drew tides. But Diane was not seeking adoration; she sought freedom and truth, eclipsed by the growing shadows of a royal conspiracy.

The nascent lights of Valoria transformed into an opal veil draping the streets in mystery and promise. For Diane, each dawn was an anthem to bravery, a bittersweet melody mixed with hope and apprehension. Under the cover of her hood, she was a whisper among the echoes of the day's beginning, her royal beauty a flickering glow in the morning mist. Her quest for truth and freedom, like a rebellious flame, refused to be smothered by the darkness of a conspiracy enveloping the throne of Valoria.

At the edge of the city, where the last houses bid farewell to the undulating fields and open trails, Diane reached the south gate. There, she paused for a moment, her gaze tenderly sweeping over the silhouettes of the sleeping buildings, as if to carry with her the memory of each stone and every alley. And it was there, in this silent contemplation, that another figure appeared on the horizon, capturing the princess's attention with an almost unreal elegance.

The figure moved with an ease that defied the whisper of the breezes, each motion imbued with wild grace and a fluidity that betrayed a perfect mastery of body and space. Diane, whose sharp mind could discern greatness in the shadow of a step, knew that such a gait belonged only to those who had embraced wandering, to those whose eyes had learned to read the secrets of the woods and plains. Without a sound, without hesitation, she chose to follow this silent dance, driven by an intuition whispering to her that this stranger might be the key to her uncertain journey.

What Diane couldn't guess was that the stranger was none other than Iris, whose reputation was not that of a mere traveler, but that of a shadow among the living, a whisper extinguishing the candles of existence. She didn't know that the grace she so admired was forged in the flames of an entirely different destiny, that of a sharp blade seeking truth in the darkness of souls.

In the tableau of dawn, the destinies of the rose and the lily were about to intertwine, their paths ready to converge in a delicate dance of circumstance and choice. And it was in this silent ballet that the rebel princess followed the assassin, unaware that the next step might be her last.

The ambush was a whisper of wind, a shadow separating from the others. Diane found herself face to face with the embodiment of her own desire for adventure, a cold blade, and a silent question hanging between them. But when the hood fell, revealing the angelic face of the princess, time seemed to halt its flight. Iris's sword wavered, hesitant, while Diane's blue eyes reflected hope and urgency.

Iris, lowering her weapon, eyed warily, "What drives a princess to leave the safety of her walls, alone and unescorted?"

Diane, with resolved vulnerability, replied, "I flee a web woven of lies and enchantments. My mother, the queen, is prisoner to an illusion I cannot shatter alone. I need to reach the city of mages, for only their knowledge can lift the veil that has blinded the throne."

With a half-smile, Iris retorted, "And why follow me in such an indiscreet manner?" Her question, laced with a hint of amusement, betrayed a sense of security in the face of Diane's clumsy tailing, a reassuring contrast to the usual dangers of her assassin's world.

Recognizing the hint of sarcasm in Iris's voice, Diane responded, "The moment I saw you, I knew you were different. An adventurer, perhaps a ranger or a hunter. And who better to trace the safest path to the next inn? I thought following you would be my best asset to leave the city incognito, away from the overly curious eyes that might prevent me from departing."

Her expression, a mix of seriousness and a hint of challenge, revealed a more complex side of the princess, blending vulnerability and a form of pragmatic cunning.

Iris, with a touch of curiosity in her sharp gaze, observed the princess carefully before responding: "To the next inn it is, then. I accept to play the role of your sword, princess, until our next stop." She let out a half-smile, mixing irony and amusement. "I wouldn't want you to fall into the clutches of goblins along the way."

Then, her expression turned more serious, her gaze clouded by a shadow reflecting echoes of her own past: "As for me, I too am seeking answers at the city of mages. But unlike you, who fight to restore a situation, I seek a radical change. I'm not going there to restore order, but to sever definitively the ties of a past that haunts me."

"Your sword and your courage are what I need," Diane said with a smile tinged with gratitude and hope, "But don't think I ask you to bear the weight of our journey alone. I may be without armor, but my words and my knowledge of the lands of the empire are worth their weight in gold. Every city, every village, I know them like the back of my hand."

Iris, looking at Diane, evaluating not only the proposition but the princess herself, "Then, we would unite our strengths... You, the diplomat and negotiator, me, the armed arm of our unlikely duo."

Diane nodded, a new determination shining in her eyes. "Together, we are stronger. More capable of eluding dangers and deciphering the riddles that await us."

Iris, a mysterious smile playing on her lips, "I accept, not for the promise of a fruitful alliance, but because I see in you a spark... a spark that might well illuminate the shadows of our respective paths."

The decision was made, sealing their shared destiny. In the depths of Iris's mind, it was the undeniable beauty of Diane, a beauty not superficial but emanating from her spirit and heart, that had influenced her judgment. And as they prepared to walk side by side, Iris vowed to safeguard this nascent partnership, curious to see how the princess would prove her worth in the arena of the real world.

A pact was forged in the secrecy of dawn, a silent agreement between the noble fugitive and the solitary warrior. Together, they would take the southern road. They would be accomplices in the quest for truth, bound by fate and a growing trust. At least until the next inn.

And so began their journey, in the shadow of the trees of Valoria, under the watchful gaze of the statues of ancient heroes, on the Bridge of Legends, witnesses to the alliance of two valiant souls.

On The Way To Valdor!

The dialogue resumed as the morning shadows stretched over the paths still fresh with the morning dew.

Iris, her eye scanning the distant horizon: "So, omniscient princess, what path does your wisdom prescribe to reach Seranthea? Through the mire of the Aboreus swamps, perhaps, or by scaling the merciless peaks of the Tianzi mountains?"

Diane, unfolding an imaginary map before her eyes: "Under normal circumstances, the seductive blue of the Valoria Sea would have carried us to Stellarae, on the edge of our destination. However, Lysandra Thorne, the supreme commander of the Imperial Golden Guard, has decided that the sea is no longer a free path. She has tightened the net around the ports for weeks. Even the seagulls seem to shy away from their waters." She continued, "The most sensible course for us would be to reach Valdor on the shores of the azure lake. It's a village nestled in the embrace of the hills, where the clear waters can offer us respite and resources. We could stock up on provisions there and, with some luck, convince a hardened mercenary to join our quest, before crossing the purple steppes, where brigands lurk like hungry wolves in the shadows."

Iris listened, a half-smile softening the usually stern features of her face. "Three days' walk, you say? And here I find myself relying on the knowledge of a princess. It seems you are more than just a crownable travel companion."

Diane, a light laugh escaping her lips, "I told you so, Iris. I am not without resources. And as for Valdor, you'll find it's a wise choice. They have the best mead you can taste and beds that will make you forget the harshness of the roads."

Iris, nodding, impressed despite herself, "Then off to Valdor we go. For the mead, the comfortable beds... and yes, perhaps even a mercenary or two. After all, even a shadow can appreciate the warmth of a welcoming inn."

A tacit agreement seemed to have woven itself between them, silently extending the bonds of their shared adventure beyond the walls of the first inn.

Their dialogue resonated with the promise of

a balanced partnership, challenges to face, and adventures to come. The two women set off, leaving behind the deceptive safety of Valoria to plunge into the arms of the unknown, where each road, each village, and each encounter could shape them and prepare them for what awaited in the vast world that lay before them.

Their silhouettes cut across the horizon as Diane and Iris ventured beyond the borders of Valoria, following the winding path that would lead them to Valdor. The first day of walking enveloped them in a cloak of greenery; trees leaned over their path, forming a living tunnel under which they advanced. Iris, accustomed to the harshness of the elements, moved with unshakable assurance, while Diane, despite her inexperience with foot travel, displayed endurance and determination that commanded respect.

As night fell, they set up a makeshift camp under the sparkling veil of bold stars that dared defy the depth of the nocturnal sky. As Diane struggled to set up her bedding with unconvincing grace, an amused smile appeared on Iris's lips. This smile was exchanged for practical advice, and soon, a fire crackled, warming their bodies and hearts. When the princess attempted to prepare a travel meal, the results were comically unrefined but eaten with gratitude. The difference in their worlds revealed itself in these simple gestures, but a mutual respect began to weave a solid bond between them.

On the second day, they crossed fields of undulating wheat that danced to the rhythm of a gentle breeze, seemingly guiding them towards their destination. Diane shared stories of each hamlet and stream they encountered, while Iris listened, her mind usually focused on survival, opening to the richness of a world she had often overlooked. In the evening, they shared tales of their lives, melodies of their dreams, finding in the symphony of crickets and the crackling of wood a melody for their own emerging legends.

On the third day, dawn found them already on the path, the rising sun painting the world in warm colors and gold. The shared laughter at Diane's accidental fall or Iris's grimace at the sweetness of a wild berry became the light notes of their journey.

Sometimes, mysterious affinities wove together, creating the illusion of knowing each other for an eternity after only a few hours shared. Here were two souls that everything seemed to oppose, two destinies that should never have crossed, and yet, a common fate brought them together, weaving between them the threads of an unexpected friendship.

* * *

The Secrets

As they neared the last kilometers to the village of Valdor, Diane and Iris walked under a serene sky, dialogue weaving between them with newfound ease.

Diane, with a dreamy air: "Normally, a perfect group of adventurers also includes a mage, a warrior, and a healing priest. With that, crossing the purple steppes would be child's play."

Iris, her piercing skepticism: "A warrior, certainly. But a mage and a priest in that inn? It's not a capital tavern or an adventurers' guild. And I have my reservations about mages."

Diane, a crystalline laugh escaping her lips: "I never imagined a ranger could be so wary. To see you, one might think you're a paranoid ranger, if I count the number of rabbits and other nocturnal visitors that nearly met their end."

Iris, a fleeting smile lighting up her face: "That's how I am. Between living and dying, sometimes there's only a second."

Their conversation was abruptly interrupted by the

appearance of two unsavory-looking individuals, clad in light armor, suggesting apprentice brigands or mere thugs. One of them, advancing with misplaced arrogance, blocked their path.

Brigand, in a honeyed and provocative tone: "What are two charming ladies doing alone on this road? It's hardly prudent. Let us teach you how to get acquainted."

Diane, opening her mouth to retort, was interrupted by the flash of a blade. In an instant, Iris had her sword under the throat of the impertinent man, her icy gaze piercing his soul.

Iris, in a low and threatening voice: "Pretty women can be head-turning... The next time we cross paths, that's likely what will happen."

The two men, terrified, took off running, one of them leaving an embarrassing stain on his pants.

Diane, breathlessly: "Iris, sometimes you can be frightening! Have you ever solved a problem without putting your blade under someone's throat?"

Iris, simply: "No."

Diane, a shiver in her voice: "Since we are on the topic of violence, it's time I confided something about my hasty departure. You must have been wondering why my quest was so urgent…"

She then took out a black rose from her bag, a symbol both ominous and mysterious.

Diane: "You know what this is, don't you? Everyone knows its meaning…"

Iris, her gaze darkening: "Fate is playful… Diane, there is also something you should know. You are not traveling with just any ranger, but with Iris Blackthorn, the 'Shadowdancer', an elite member of the Black Roses until three days ago. I decided to run, to flee from death. Simply, I run to no longer give it."

Diane shuddered at the revelation. The Shadowdancer, a legend among assassins, was traveling by her side. She remembered the words of Commander Thorne: "Shadowdancer, what a loss for the Black Roses to have such an agile fighter. She would have her place in my elite units."

Iris then shared with Diane the story of her stolen life, of her childhood taken to serve a merciless organization. Diane, listening with compassion and astonishment, felt an even stronger bond forming between them.

As the sun began to set while they neared Valdor,

each now carried the other's secret. Together, they moved towards the village, united by a newfound trust and a deepened mutual understanding, ready to face the challenges and mysteries that the future held for them.

With faces marked by wind and sun, they approached the welcoming lights of the inn, ready to savor the well-deserved rest. This journey had been a time of mutual discovery, where the princess and the assassin had learned to see beyond titles and masks, finding in their diversity a common strength, and in their union, a foretaste of what a true alliance could be.

CHAPTER 3: THE DARKNESS OF ELYSORIUM

Naragath

Many days' journey from Valdor, far from fertile lands and dazzling cities, lay the mysterious realm of Naragath, with its vast desert of sand. Here, whimsical winds sculpted shifting dunes, writing the ephemeral chronicles of the sand kingdoms, tales that renewed with each dawn and dissolved under the stars. This desert, a stage for forgotten legends, appeared as a living parchment where nature endlessly wrote and erased its stories.

At the far west of Naragath, Lunaris stood, majestic and solitary, a dark gem polished by the ages. It was the beacon of the west, overseeing the horizon opposite Solara, its luminous twin. Lunaris, nicknamed the 'Gate of Hell', rose in this infernal paradise, with its bold towers clawing at the night sky, flirting with the stars. The city's walls, built of dark stones, seemed to swallow the daylight, revealing only silver reflections under the moonlight, like whispers of a forgotten goddess.

In the heart of Lunaris, the market was a

kaleidoscope of life. A thousand and one voices rose, carrying echoes from distant and unknown lands. The alleyways twisted into a mysterious labyrinth, where each turn offered a new enigma, a new tale, a new adventure to be discovered.

To the east, the desert stretched, vast and mysterious, interrupted only by the sinister shadow of 'The Crucible'. This stronghold of the necromancer Astaroth Soulreaver stood as a monument to forbidden power, a temple of dark arts where the accusatory fingers of the towers seemed to defy the heavens, and the windows, lit with a supernatural glow, lay in wait for the souls of lost travelers.

Between Lunaris and 'The Crucible', the land offered a tapestry of illusions and realities, of dangers and sanctuaries. The Oasis of Reprieve, with its pure waters and palm trees whispering ancient melodies, was a haven of peace in this merciless world. Further on, in Duskarn, there were whispers of encounters with entities from the darkest legends, beings whose very mention stirred fear and wonder.

At the far east of Naragath, the Dark Tower dominated the landscape, a mysterious and isolated edifice, a sanctuary for black mages and guardian of forgotten secrets. There, the sand took on the colors of the night, and magic permeated the air, weaving a veil between the real and the imaginary, between what is and what might be.

Naragath thus revealed itself, a landscape of cruel and enchanting beauty, where each dune resonated with ancient enchantments and every breath of wind carried echoes of a bygone era. In this arid and majestic land, legends took deep root, defying time and memory, weaving a narrative that renewed itself with each sunset, opening the doors to the infinite.

❈ ❈ ❈

Dark Designs

In the arid and desolate heart of Naragath's desert, a dark scheme was brewing, casting a sinister web over the fate of Elysorium. In this inhospitable region, "The Crucible" stood as a bastion of terror. The tower of Astaroth Soulreaver, the feared necromancer, built of black stones eroded by time and ash storms, absorbed the dull light of the sky, creating around it a halo of darkness, where its summit was lost in the low, tumultuous clouds.

Howling winds made ashes and dust dance in a macabre ballet, enveloping the landscape in a fatal veil. The earth itself seemed to groan under the burden of secrets and curses locked within the tower. Nowhere else in Naragath - except perhaps in Duskarn - was such a concentration of dark and mysterious energy felt.

At the foot of the sinister tower, a wrought-iron gate adorned with esoteric symbols seldom opened. But on that day, it creaked on its hinges, heralding the arrival of a most formidable visitor: Sarthax, the Black General. This imposing warrior, clad in black dragon-scale armor, was a vision of terror incarnate. Each step he took on the barren ground echoed like an omen of desolation.

A member of the order of black paladins, Sarthax had forsaken the divine light to embrace the darkness. Once protectors of faith and justice, these fallen knights had traded their devotion for allegiance to malevolent entities, becoming incarnations of terror and power.

Advancing towards the tower, Sarthax cleaved the oppressive silence with his heavy steps. The shadow creatures, usually masters of these desolate places, instinctively recoiled before his menacing aura. Known as 'Mage Killers' for their hostility towards practitioners of the mystical arts, these black paladins were feared by all who wielded magic.

The presence of Sarthax at The Crucible was a bad omen, signaling sinister plans and a power ambition that boded ill. Inside the tower, the walls were covered with cobwebs and shelves laden with strange artifacts and black magic grimoires. The light from the torches with their bluish flame cast unsettling shadows, seeming to whisper ancient secrets. The air was imbued with a musty odor of incense, a bewitching mix that aroused the senses in an almost supernatural way.

At the top of the tower, under a stone dome in a circular room, Astaroth Soulreaver waited, draped in a long black robe, his face concealed by a hood. His eyes glowed with an unsettling light, and around him floated luminous orbs, illuminating the scrolls and artifacts spread out before him. The silence of the room was broken by the creaking of the gate opening below. Astaroth looked up, an enigmatic smile on his lips. "Sarthax..." he murmured in a chilling voice. 'The pieces are beginning to fall into place."

In the sinister depths of the tower, the powerful and deep voice of Sarthax echoed, breaking the heavy silence that enveloped the room. "Necromancer,'" he began, his deep tone imbuing each word with gravity, "The city of Lunaris is ours. Cassandra, who rules it in our name, will ensure that no mage comes snooping into our affairs. The only gateway to this part of the continent is now closed."

Astaroth Soulreaver, a shadow among shadows, replied in an ethereal voice, as if emerging from the beyond, 'Excellent news, General. Nothing now seems to hinder the return of the Dragon Emperor. Eva and Pandora are busy gathering the last elements necessary for the ritual…"

Sarthax, slightly furrowing his brows, continued, 'These demonesses are unpredictable. But exploiting their power is tempting. I will head north to Misthall to ensure our gold supply."

Soulreaver, with a cold smile forming on his lips, retorted, "When the Emperor awakens, material concerns will be a thing of the past.."

Sarthax, pragmatic, replied, "In the meantime, gold remains essential for buying loyalty and influence. Wars are won with steel and gold."

After a silence heavy with implications, Sarthax asked, "Any news of Valoria?" His piercing gaze, from under his helmet, scrutinized Soulreaver intensely.

"Morgana controls the queen, ensuring our discretion in the city. She also leads the Black Roses, eliminating our enemies through her assassins. The princess is doomed; her death will only increase Morgana's grip on the queen. replied Soulreaver, his eyes twinkling with a cunning delight.

A sinister laugh escaped from Soulreaver, its echoes mingling with the shadows of the room. "The princess... what a pity not to have offered her to the succubi," he added with undisguised cruelty.

The conversation between these two dark figures was charged with a palpable threat, each word and silence weaving a sinister and desolate future for Elysorium. Their alliance was a pact tied in the depths of darkness, a macabre understanding. Finally, Sarthax rose, his armor clinking sinisterly. He turned his back on Soulreaver and moved towards the exit, his silhouette gradually fading into the darkness of the corridor, leaving behind an atmosphere charged with ill intentions and diabolical plots.

❊ ❊ ❊

CHAPTER 4: THE ARCANE PEARL

At The Inn

In the heart of the Golden Valley, where the gentle waters of the Azure Lake softly kiss the shores, lies the village of Valdor. Flanked to the west by the daunting peaks of the Griffin's Spire and to the east by the Tianzi Mountains, majestic-like celestial columns reminiscent of an ancient painting, Valdor nestles like a jewel on the azure cradle of the lake. This haven attracts travelers seeking rest, with its harmoniously scattered houses around the lake, built of stone and wood from the surrounding forests, symbols of the union between man and nature. The village, living to the rhythm of the seasons, harvests, fishermen, and artisans, becomes a refuge for lost souls fleeing distant conflicts and adventurers in search of fame, thus offering a place of harmony and perhaps a new beginning.

After three days of walking, Diane and Iris finally beheld Valdor spread out before them. Under the golden light of dusk, the tranquil waters of the lake mirrored a peaceful scene, while the streets, alive with a serene bustle, echoed with the comings and goings of the villagers at day's end. Upon their arrival at the Valdor inn, they were enveloped by the warmth of flames dancing in the fireplace and the appetizing aromas of simmering dishes. The murmur of conversations, punctuated by the laughter of the locals, wove a warm and inviting atmosphere. Approaching the counter, they were greeted by a jovial innkeeper, whose broad and welcoming smile promised hospitality and comfort.

Upon entering, the innkeeper greeted them warmly. "Welcome to the Lake Inn! What can I do for you, ladies?" he asked.

Diane, exhausted but smiling, replied, "We would like a room for the night, and perhaps something to eat." The innkeeper led them to a cozy room upstairs and then to a table near the window, offering a soothing view of the lake shimmering under the last rays of the setting sun.

As they dined, the conversation between Diane and Iris became more intimate. "Does it not scare you to travel with an assassin?" asked Iris.

Diane, with a contemplative look, answered, "To be honest, it's rather exciting. And I feel reassured having you by my side, Iris. Your skill is a real asset. I keep thinking about the crestfallen faces of our assailants."

Iris, showing a sincere smile, added: "I am also happy with our alliance. Even though you are a bit more talkative than my usual companions." Their shared laughter filled the inn, creating a relaxed and warm atmosphere.

Having finished their meal, Diane, with eyes sparkling with amusement, remarked, "Look, I've spotted some interesting people. What do you think of that dwarf with his imposing axe?"

Iris shook her head, a half-smile on her face. "Dwarves? They're a bit too headstrong for my liking. And what about that ranger at the counter? His scars tell tales of distant and dangerous lands…"

Diane replied playfully, "Iris, we're trying to recruit companions to protect us from people like him, actually." Their camaraderie intensified, their laughter rising above the hubbub of the inn.

Suddenly, Diane's gaze fell on a hooded figure at a secluded table. "Him, over there, in the shadow of the candles… A scout, or perhaps a bounty hunter?" she whispered.

Iris followed Diane's gaze and studied the figure carefully. "Look at the cloak… finely hemmed with mithril thread. That's not the gear of an ordinary adventurer. A noble on the run, or a mage, I'd wager," she concluded, a hint of suspicion in her voice.

Diane nodded, her eyes narrowing. "He stands out in this rustic den. A priest, or a scholar of the arcane, perhaps?" Their curiosity piqued, they stood up, ready to uncover the secrets of this enigmatic presence.

※ ※ ※

The Eternal Student

Approaching the hooded figure, Diane spoke with diplomacy: "Good evening. Your cloak suggests you are not from here. We are headed to Seranthea and seek traveling companions. Would you be interested in a shared journey?" When the stranger revealed her face, a young mage with eyes sparkling with intelligence and curiosity appeared. Despite her youth, the depth of her gaze betrayed a surprising maturity and sagacity.

Tilting her head with a relaxed air, the young mage asked: "I might be heading to Seranthea myself. But you, you don't quite look like mages… Is it the wind of adventure that drives you, or circumstances that compel you?"

Diane took a breath, weighing her words carefully: "An audience with an archmage is imperative for an urgent matter concerning the royalty of Valoria."

Her voice carried the weight of their quest.

With a wry smile, the mage retorted, "Just that? Is this mission official? Under whose auspices do you operate?"

Iris, with a chill in her voice, quickly corrected, "Her authority is sufficient, she is Princess Diane of Valoria. She needs no one's approval." Althea appeared surprised, her eyes shining with renewed interest.

"And you," she inquired, scrutinizing Iris, "hardly look like a princess's companion..."

Iris answered candidly, her voice tinged with dark determination, "I need to gather information about my past from the mages... and I intend to eliminate Astaroth Soulreaver, a formidable dark mage, before he awakens an abyssal dragon." At the mention of Astaroth, the young mage flinched, recognizing the name.

The mage laughed openly, "You, with your braided hair and serious air, would take on the necromancer?"

Iris's irritation was palpable, "You seem well-informed. Suspicious, don't you think?"

She shook her head, a mischievous smile on her lips. "What mage worth their salt wouldn't know the necromancer? But tell me, what has this sinister character done for you to decide to traverse the whole country in search of him?"

Iris, with a hint of bitterness, revealed: "He is said to have kidnapped my mother, tortured her for his unholy rituals, and made me the puppet of an assassin's sect. Delightful, isn't it?" Surprise painted itself again on the face of the mage, who seemed to know more than she let on.

After a brief reflection, the mage announced playfully, "I will accompany you to Seranthea. Not to assist in your quest, but because the idea of these 'entertaining' stories of a lady of the court and a huntress waging war against a dragon intrigues me." She leaned back in her chair, an anticipatory smile lighting up her face. "I'm eager to hear the rest of your 'jokes'. But for now, let's savor this exquisite wine." Pouring the wine, she introduced herself: "Althea, is my name. I am an eternal student of the mage's guild."

Diane exclaimed with enthusiasm. "Fantastic! We now have a mage in our team!"

Iris tempered Diane's excitement, "Don't be too hopeful, she said student..." A hint of disappointment showed in her voice.

The newly formed trio concluded their meal with laughter and a toast to their improbable alliance. Althea, with her skepticism and sharp wit, offered a new dynamic to the duo of Diane and Iris. Their journey to Seranthea now promised to be rich in sparkling interactions and unexpected challenges.

❈ ❈ ❈

About To Leave

At dawn, the Lake Inn of Valdor awoke under the soft light of the rising sun, which made its way through the windows, painting a ballet of shadows and lights on the old wooden floors. The rays landed on the tables, illuminating the grains of wood worn by time, and made the dust dance in the air, like miniature stars floating in an inner cosmos. The warmth of the hearth - which had simmered gently all night - continued to radiate its comfort, inviting the early risers to linger in its warm embrace.

Diane, Iris, and Althea, forming an unlikely alliance in the wake of the previous evening's events, gathered for a well-deserved breakfast. The tables of the inn, polished by the tales of passing travelers, welcomed them with their almost maternal warmth. The common room, bathed in the serenity of the first rays of the day, offered a welcome respite from the tumult of their recent adventures. Around their table, the trio indulged in an assortment of fresh breads, whose golden crusts crackled under the bite, aromatic local cheeses, whose scents tantalized the palate, and juicy fruits straight from the enchanted forests of Stellarae, whose vibrant colors awakened the spirit as much as the taste. The room was filled with the appetizing scents of morning cooking, where the aromas of strong coffee and fresh herbs mingled in an olfactory dance that promised a day full of hope.

Diane, always driven by insatiable curiosity, turned to Althea, determination clearly readable in her green eyes that sparkled with a mischievous glint. "Althea, what is your specialty in magic? Can you, for example, roast our enemies, conjure up storms, or transform into a bear?" she asked, her interest ringing in her voice like the melody of a well-tuned lute. She bit into a piece of crispy bread, her white teeth contrasting with the golden crumb, demonstrating a joie de vivre that seemed unshakable even in the face of adversity.

Althea, a mysterious smile on her lips, took a sip of her tea, whose vapors rose like morning mists over a tranquil valley. Her eyes sparkling with intelligence and mischief, she replied with a voice that carried the nuances of an ancient melody, both soft and powerful. "As I mentioned last night, I am an eternal student of the arcane. The diversity of my knowledge is my greatest asset, and my motto is 'Just the right amount of magic, no more, no less.'"

Iris, dressed in crafted leathers that hugged her

athletic form, bore the marks of her numerous battles. She was attentive, observing Althea. The warrior said, "You travel alone, dressed so elegantly. Student or not, you seem perfectly at ease on the road. And confident about your safety." she said, her tone tinged with a slight skepticism but also a growing respect. Iris had learned to read people, to see beyond appearances, and something about Althea fascinated her, almost as much as it put her on guard.

Althea met her gaze, a glimmer of wisdom and a hint of mystery in her eyes. "Knowledge is a form of protection, that's true. I have some useful tricks for traveling," she replied, her voice as clear and melodious as the sound of a crystal bell, "but there's also the tacit knowledge that every mage accumulates over the years. A knowledge that resides not only in the mind but also in the heart."

Their breakfast unfolded in an atmosphere of mutual curiosity and respect. The walls of the inn, silent witnesses to so many stories, seemed to absorb every word, every laugh, as if to weave them into the great tapestry of time. As Diane and Iris shared their experiences, Althea listened attentively, her comments sprinkled with humor and insight. It was an exchange of lives, dreams, and fears, a sharing that rarely occurred among strangers, but which, in the span of a morning, had transformed them into travel companions.

Diane, unable to resist, asked with a hint of eagerness, "Althea, tell us about one of your adventures. Are there spells or artifacts that have left a mark on you?" Her question was an invitation to share their stories and knowledge, a desire to understand not just the mysteries of the world, but also those traveling alongside her.

Althea smiled, letting her thoughts travel back in time to places shrouded in mist and legend. "I have explored ancient ruins, deciphered forgotten texts, and encountered creatures of legend. Each discovery has taught me that magic is a window into the mysteries of our world, much more than just a series of spells. I've seen artifacts that could divert the course of a river, or grimoires so ancient that merely reading them could change you forever."

The breakfast continued in a spirit of sharing and discovery. Each brought her own perspective, weaving a bond of camaraderie and mutual appreciation. This meal marked not only the start of a new day but also the beginning of a shared adventure, where each would contribute her strengths and knowledge to face the challenges on the road to Seranthea. It was a moment suspended in time, a precious instant where the past and the future converged, wrapped in a present that promised to unite them against the shadows to come.

OLIVIER ELOPHE

* * *

CHAPTER 5: AN IMPORTANT MISSION

In The Archmage's Tower

A few days earlier, in Etheal, at the highest mage tower of the city of Seranthea, a crucial dialogue was taking place between Althea Etherend and the archmage Valerius, the dean of archmages. The top of the tower offered a breathtaking view of the glittering city below, but inside, it was an entirely different world. The walls were lined with shelves filled with ancient grimoires and mysterious artifacts, evidence of centuries of accumulated knowledge. Orbs of light floated gently, illuminating the room with a supernatural glow.

Althea entered with respect. 'You summoned me, Archmage Valerius?'

Valerius, looking out the window, turned towards her. "Althea, I have a mission of the utmost importance for you. And as always, it must remain confidential."

"I am ready to listen."

Valerius continued, "You are to go to the imperial prison of Thorneira. Give this note to the garrison commander to access the high-security tower. I would like you to interrogate the fallen archmage Thalios."

Surprised, Althea responded, "It must be serious to address that traitor."

Valerius nodded, "The situation is worrying. Thalios was leading Lunaris before being exposed for his dark machinations. We have discovered he was accumulating forbidden artifacts and practicing dark powers."

"As the keeper of forbidden knowledge, I remember his misdeeds well," Althea reminisced

"It is for your intelligence and adaptability that I turn to you. We have detected ancient magical energies in Naragath, and several priests of light have disappeared. I have a bad feeling."

"The necromancer Astaroth Soulreaver, do you think?" Althea questioned.

Valerius considered, "Possible, there are rumors about his quest to recall the dragon emperor. But Soulreaver lacks the logistics for that."

Althea resolved, "I will leave immediately."

"Perfect. On my end, I will meet with Queen Cassandra in Lunaris. She is a valued and admired ally, surrounded by popular legends. I want to ensure that Naragath remains under surveillance." Valerius continued, "Upon your return, stop by

Mirela at the temple of Solis. Let's make sure she's well."

"With pleasure," Althea replied, "And you, be careful in Lunaris. Far too many rumors are reaching us from Naragath these days.."

Althea left the room, her mind already focused on the mission ahead. As she descended the spiral stairs of the tower, she pondered the challenges that awaited her, the secrets she might uncover, and the inherent dangers of confronting a fallen mage like Thalios. The mission was perilous, but Althea Etherend was a mage not only talented, but also fearless, ready to face the shadows to unveil the truth.

Fate had woven its web, preparing the ground for a journey that would take Althea from the ethereal heights of magical knowledge to the sinister and dangerous depths of the imperial prison.

The imperial prison stood in an austere place, where the elements themselves seemed to be the guardians of its isolation. To the west, the relentless waves of the ocean beat against its walls, as if to remind of the unattainable freedom. To the south, the intimidating peaks of the Twin Dragon range stood, a natural bulwark against the outside world, while to the east, the Griffin Peaks extended their stone wings, watching over this fortress of despair.

To reach this citadel of shadow, one would have to travel through the Golden Valley, head north of the Azure Lake, and cross lands dotted with plant gold and light, a poignant contrast to the fate of the souls locked within. Several days' march separated Seranthea from this bastille, and each step would be a move away from the wisdom of the mages to draw closer to the icy whisper of chains and the silence of the cells.

❖ ❖ ❖

Althea In Seranthea

Althea Etherend left the tower of the archmage Valerius, her thoughts swirling around the entrusted mission. As she descended the ancient stone steps, she soon found herself in the lively streets of Seranthea, the beating heart of magic in Etheal. The city, a true crossroads of knowledge and mysteries, unfolded before her in all its splendor.

The paved streets of Seranthea were lined with majestic buildings, their facades adorned with magical symbols and frescoes depicting mythical scenes. The mage towers, tall and slender, stood proudly, piercing the sky with their glittering summits. Their stained glass cast mosaics of colored light on the cobblestones, telling stories of bygone eras and battles against dark forces.

The city's markets brimmed with merchants selling exotic potion ingredients, energy crystals, and ancient artifacts. Mages in shimmering robes mingled with curious apprentices and city dwellers, creating a living mosaic of magical society. The hanging gardens of Seranthea, a masterpiece of engineering and magic, offered a sanctuary of peace and natural beauty, where rare plants and enchanted flowers thrived under the watchful care of mage-gardeners.

Althea headed to her abode to prepare for the journey. Her residence, located near the academic libraries, was a place of tranquility and reflection. She gathered her essential belongings: scrolls, inks, a few selected grimoires, ingredients for basic spells, and travel-suited clothing. She also checked her magical equipment: a staff adorned with runes, a cloak woven with mithril threads, and protective amulets. Each item was chosen carefully, reflecting her meticulous preparation and deep knowledge of magic.

Before leaving, Althea spent a moment in the private sanctuary of her home, a small room dedicated to meditation and magical contemplation. Here, surrounded by crystals and sacred symbols, she focused on the energies around her, seeking strength and wisdom for the challenges ahead. She performed a final check of her magical protections, ensuring she was ready to face the potential dangers of her mission.

Leaving Seranthea, Althea crossed the city gates with quiet determination. She knew that the journey to the imperial prison would not be without risks, but she was resolved to fulfill the task entrusted to her by Archmage Valerius. Her mind was clear, her heart ready for the adventure, and her steps carried her inexorably towards the destiny that awaited her on the road.

Althea, bearing the weight of a mission entrusted by Archmage Valerius, began her journey across the vast landscapes of Elysorium. On the morning of her departure, the rising sun painted the sky with fiery colors, promising a day full of discoveries and magic.

❋ ❋ ❋

The Crystal Plains

To the east of Seranthea lie the majestic Crystal Plains, whose fame spreads well beyond the borders of Elysorium. A vast expanse where nature has orchestrated a symphony of purplish-pink hues, these magical crystals spring from the ground in a dazzling display. They emerge in delicate formations here and there, some even reaching heights greater than a man, like giants frozen in eternal contemplation of the sky.

The magical energy that permeates these plains is so intense that it becomes almost tangible, vibrating around visitors like the beating of an ancient and powerful heart. This force, as enchanting as it is, can only be tolerated for a few precious minutes by the uninitiated; most travelers thus choose to marvel at this surreal beauty by respectfully bypassing it, not daring to disturb its tranquility.

Only a few mages, masters of their art, have the privilege to walk freely among the crystallizations, moving with ease through this enchanted labyrinth. They are the guardians of these mysteries, and they alone are able to listen and understand the harmonious song of the crystals which, under the effect of the wind, seem to whisper ancient incantations and reveal the secrets of a forgotten world.

In the heart of the Crystal Plains, Althea Etherend walked with serene steps, enveloped by the tranquility of the place. The twilight light lazily stretched over the sparkling carpet of gems, bathing the horizon in perpetual luminescence. Each crystal, a node in the living network of Elysorium's magic, sang at a frequency that resonated to the soul of the mage.

She felt the power of the crystals vibrate deep within her being, a symphony of nature that strengthened her intimate connection with the arcane arts of magic. Althea had once been nicknamed "the Crystal Mage" for her unique ability to harmonize and manipulate these magical resonances.

At dusk, Althea prepared her camp with precision and attention that betrayed her knowledge of elemental forces. She raised a subtle barrier of crystalline illuminations, not for protection – for few dared to challenge a mage of her stature – but for the pure beauty of the act. The crystals around her, silent witnesses to her ritual, sparkled in response to her enchantments.

Before falling asleep, leaning against her backpack serving as a pillow, she contemplated the stars. Her mind wandered to her responsibilities as the Guardian of Forbidden Magic, a title heavy with meaning and danger. Her studies had led her to decipher grimoires veiled in mystery, texts that even the archmages themselves were wary of.

Althea, a sage incarnate, never allowed herself to be seduced by the intoxication of power. She knew that wisdom did not reside in the demonstration of force, but in restraint, in the art of using magic only with discernment and necessity. And yet, Archmage Valerius himself had described her magical potential as "dizzying". A power she carefully kept under control, aware of the fine line that separates wisdom from excess.

The night settled in, and Althea, under the sparkling dome woven by the constellations and the crystals, slipped into sleep. She needed to rest, to recenter herself, for the next day, she would resume her journey towards the imperial prison, where a fallen archmage awaited, a man who might hold the keys to mysteries threatening the entire kingdom. Her mission was clear, and her mind, despite the fatigue, remained focused on the imminent challenge.

❋ ❋ ❋

The Crimson Steppes

The next day, Althea resumed her journey to the next stop, an inn known as the Four Winds Inn, located on the south shore of White Lake. The inn was a popular spot for travelers and merchants, as well as crystal seekers and mages who came to study the unique properties of the region.

The building was constructed with translucent quartz blocks, and inside, each room was lit by lamps filled with crystal powder, providing a soothing and rejuvenating light. The innkeeper, a middle-aged man with eyes sparkling with enthusiasm, greeted Althea with respectful deference, recognizing her as a mage of Seranthea.

After a nourishing meal of garden vegetables, enriched with aromatic herbs and tea infused with mint crystals, Althea took the time to talk with the locals. She listened to their stories, learning from their experiences and in return, sharing anecdotes about life in Seranthea.

The night at the Crystal Inn was restorative. Althea took a moment to meditate, allowing the ambient magic of the crystals to revitalize her and sharpen her mind for the next leg of her journey.

The following morning, after a breakfast of fresh fruits and crispy bread, Althea prepared to hit the road again. Her mind was clear, her determination renewed by rest and the energies of the crystals. She paid for her room and, thanking the innkeeper for the hospitality, she crossed the threshold of the inn, ready for the next stage of her journey to Thorneira.

The mage headed north, traversing a landscape that gradually changed, becoming more austere as she neared her destination. Each step took her away from the shimmering brilliance of the Crystal Plains and closer to the secrets she was to uncover at the imperial prison.

Althea Etherend, the Arcane Prodigy, continued her journey, alone amidst the wonders and mysteries of Elysorium, her story weaving into the grand narrative of her world.

As she left the Crystal Inn, Althea Etherend felt the morning chill and the humidity in the air due to the proximity of the lake. The path to the crimson steppes was dotted with frosted blades of grass and sparkling dewdrops. On the horizon, the steppes unfolded before her, vast and open, under a sky that began to be draped with clouds.

Passing not far from the temple of Solis, Althea let her gaze linger on the peaceful silhouette of the sanctuary. She thought of Mirela, the priestess she was eager to see again. "Soon," she thought to herself, a gentle smile on her lips.

But the tranquility of the journey was abruptly interrupted. Bandits, ambushed among the tall grass, sprang onto her path with clear malicious intent. Althea reacted with striking speed. With a gesture, she whispered an incantation, and an ethereal force barrier formed around her, repelling the first attacker.

"I am not the adversary you seek," she declared, her voice carrying a chilling warning.

The bandits, underestimating the mage they saw before them, launched a more determined assault. Althea, while deftly avoiding their attacks, wove a series of offensive spells. Bursts of pure light struck their targets with surgical precision. In a few moments, the bandits were neutralized, some choosing to flee in the face of the display of magical force.

She resumed her journey, her heart beating a little faster after the adrenaline of the combat. "The path is strewn with trials," she murmured, aware that each obstacle brought her closer to her goal and strengthened her resolve.

The crimson steppes were known for their wild beauty, but also for the dangers that lurked within. As Althea traversed these vast expanses, she faced a new, unexpected challenge; a second group of bandits, led by a sorcerer with eyes as dark as moonless nights, burst onto her path.

The sorcerer, a venomous smile stretching his thin lips, spoke to her in a voice dripping with greed. "You are the mage who defeated my men... I am willing to spare you in exchange for one or two of your magical trinkets. And who knows, with such a fair day, we might even let you go free rather than take you to our camp to... enhance our collection."

Althea listened, her heart beating not with fear, but with anger at the vile proposition. In her mind, hesitation arose, the idea of letting herself be captured to aid the prisoners gripped her soul of justice. But she had a mission, a charge that suffered no delay or detour. "We shall meet again," she said calmly, her blue eyes shining with an inner light.

Under the astonished gaze of the bandits, Althea raised an arm, whispering ancient words. In a burst of translucent energy, she disappeared from their view, leaving behind a trail of magical echoes. The sorcerer growled, his frustration palpable in the air still vibrating from Althea's spell. "A coward's spell, next time, young mage, you won't have this opportunity."

Althea, reappearing at a safe distance, continued on her way, her thoughts troubled by the confrontation. The arrogance of this sorcerer, who dared to consider her as a potential slave, stung her. She, a mage of her stature, reduced to merchandise? It was the kind of thought that haunted the weak-minded, incapable of recognizing true power.

She pondered the solitude of her journey. Although this autonomy was often beneficial for her confidential missions, she couldn't help but think of those who had no choice but to hire mercenaries or adventurers to ensure their safety on these roads. "No one travels alone," was the unwritten rule of these lands.

Yet, Althea traveled alone, protected by her magic and a discretion imposed by her responsibilities. Perhaps, she thought, she might one day offer her protection to fellow travelers. But her delicate missions, her forbidden knowledge, all this weighed too heavily to involve others in the shadows of her existence.

With a sigh, Althea pushed these thoughts away. Each step brought her closer to her goal, and she could not afford to divert her attention from the task at hand. She was the Keeper of Forbidden Knowledge, and her path was one of wisdom and duty, a path traced in the stars and in the stone of the Crystal Plains from where she came.

After crossing the steppes, Althea Etherend arrived in Valdor. The village, a crucial stop on her itinerary, was only a preamble to her visit to the imperial prison. She walked through the calm streets of the village, its robust buildings a testament to the ancient history of this place.

✣ ✣ ✣

The Mission

Approaching the inn, Althea introduced herself under the guise of a healer, a subtle ruse to avoid prying questions about her true identity and mission. She indicated that she had come to offer her services to the prison garrison, a story that earned her a warm welcome and no suspicious glances.

"I will be here for several days, I will need the room for that entire time," she confided to the innkeeper while handing over a few gold coins. "I'm going to visit the garrison, see if our brave soldiers need any care."

The room she was assigned was modest but clean and comfortable. She placed her belongings, her bag containing her healing instruments — or at least, what she had claimed to be such — and her travel notes. Night fell, and she rested, taking advantage of the tranquility of the inn to regain her strength.

In the morning, after a restful night's sleep and a local breakfast, she prepared for her visit to the garrison. She left behind her room and personal effects, carrying only what was necessary for her supposed healing mission.

When she arrived at the garrison, she was greeted by an atmosphere charged with military zeal. Soldiers bustled about, and the environment was marked by the characteristic rigor of the army.

Presenting Archmage Valerius's note, she was escorted through the inner courtyards to the main building.

In his austere office, the commander of the garrison, a man of imposing stature and features etched by years of service, welcomed the visitor. His graying beard lent a touch of dignity to his stern face. The walls, adorned with an array of weapons and detailed maps, bore witness to numerous battles and strategies.

Althea Etherend stood upright and confident before the war veteran. She presented the sealed letter from Archmage Valerius. The man examined it carefully, his eyebrows furrowing in incredulity and then reluctance. However, the imperial seal adorning the document compelled him to silently accept its contents. "Damned mages," he murmured, more to himself than to his guest.

"Come with me," he ordered in a tone that brooked no argument. They passed through the orderly ranks of the garrison to reach the dark cells. The commander stopped in front of Thalios' cell. "One hour, no more," he warned with icy severity. "And know that your art is futile here. Paladin seals nullify all magic. Don't attempt anything foolish; our guards are prepared for anything."

With unwavering military discipline, he left her

alone in front of the cell door, withdrawing without another word. Althea found herself face to face with Thalios, the fallen archmage, imprisoned in a silence heavy with unspoken stories and untold histories.

Thalios, who seemed but a shadow of his former self, sat in the dimness of the cell. "Who came to visit me in this cell, past those brutal guards?" His voice, though broken, still carried the echo of once-grand power.

Althea advanced, measuring each of her steps in the bare cell. "The prodigy, is it not? Valerius begins to recognize his errors," whispered Thalios, a bitter smile on his parched lips.

"I am not here to discuss my own affairs, but to find out if there is anything left of the man you were, of the honor of your mage oaths..."

"Spare me your morals, young girl. Yes, I coveted more power than was wise to possess. It's... human. Isn't that something you can understand?"

"I am here to talk about Lunaris, now led by Cassandra, and more importantly, about the necromancer. Did you deal with him to acquire the power you so desired?"

"Cassandra... Have you met her yet?" evaded Thalios, shifting the subject.

"Valerius is on his way for that. But the

necromancer... What do you know of his activities? Was there a pact between you?"

"An unspoken agreement. I did not interfere in his dark designs," replied Thalios, showing a semblance of remorse. "As for Cassandra, her eyes are wide open."

"And the Destroyer... Is the necromancer truly seeking to bring him back among us?"

"That is his ultimate goal. Why would he refrain from it?"

"And Cassandra, is she complicit through her silence?"

Thalios shrugged. "She has her own agenda as dark as her eyes are bright. And to answer your questions, Sarthax and the black paladins walk for the necromancer."

The revelation struck Althea like lightning. A chilling terror seized her, but she maintained control, masking her turmoil behind a facade of calm. Thalios, discerning her agitation, took amusement in it.

"Thank you for this information," said Althea, regaining her composure. "It will be useful."

She would have liked to delve deeper into his allegations about the new queen of Lunaris, but Althea did not want to fall into a trap of manipulation and preferred to stick to the information directly related to her subject. It was natural for Thalios to harbor resentment against Cassandra, who had precipitated his downfall.

Thalios implored, "Get me out of here, I'm locked up and treated by soldiers who hate mages. Without my magic, I'm as good as dead - their rune holds me, but not you."

With a bow of her head, she rose and left the cell, her mind swirling with the new and disturbing information. She knew that every bit of truth could be a weapon as sharp as a blade. And now she held in her hands revelations that could well shake the foundations of Elysorium.

❋ ❋ ❋

The Encounter

The troubling information revealed by the fallen archmage Thalios weighed heavily on Althea's mind as she made her way back to the inn in Valdor. Thalios's enigmatic words, laden with implications about Queen Cassandra, echoed in her head, mingling with her thoughts about the formidable black paladins, a veritable scourge for any mage.

Upon her arrival, the inn was a welcome haven after the revelations at the garrison. She took a few moments to rest in her room, allowing the weight of her mission to momentarily fade under the simple but comforting comfort of her bed. But the respite was short-lived; hunger and the need for reflection drew her to the common room for the evening meal.

Sitting at her usual table, a steaming bowl of soup before her, Althea let her gaze drift into the dancing flames of the fireplace. The warmth of the fire soothed her body while the lively ambiance of the inn caressed her spirit. It was a striking contrast to the icy cold of the truth she had learned earlier.

Suddenly, she felt heavy gazes upon her. Looking up, she saw two women at the other end of the room, an unlikely duo observing her with curiosity. One, noble and elegant despite her simplicity, and the other, of a darker and more mysterious appearance. They seemed to consult each other with their eyes before rising and approaching.

Althea watched the duo near her table. The blonde moved with the innate grace of a noblewoman, her refined gestures and confident posture perhaps betraying a diplomatic upbringing. She was likely a figure of distinction beyond the walls of a grand city. Her brunette companion, on the other hand, bore the mark of a warrior, perhaps a mercenary, a thief, or a scout. There was a tension in her eyes, a precarious balance between alertness and rest. Althea couldn't help but think that their presence was more than a mere whim of fate.

As she contemplated the bulletin board where requests for mercenaries were pinned, Althea smiled mischievously at the idea of hiring a protector for her return journey. The notion that a mage of her stature needed protection seemed amusing to her, and yet, the solitude of the road weighed on her.

As she mulled over this idea, the contrasting duo approached her. The golden-haired noblewoman spoke first, her soft voice carrying the assurance of those accustomed to being heard: "Good evening. Your cloak suggests that you are not from around here. We are traveling to Seranthea and are looking for travel companions. Would you be interested in joining us?"

Althea had to suppress a surge of enthusiasm. It was an unexpected opportunity, but she couldn't reveal her interest too quickly. "I may also be heading to Seranthea. Are you traveling for pleasure or necessity?" she asked with measured curiosity, while carefully observing her interlocutors.

Golden-haired Diane explained that she was seeking assistance for a matter concerning the royalty of Valoria. The other woman, more reserved, was named Iris, and her quest was more personal: she was searching for answers about her past.

Althea listened, her mind already weaving the threads of a potential collaboration. These women, although very different from her, shared a common goal that led them all towards Seranthea. A tacit agreement seemed to form between them, an alliance forged not only out of necessity but also by a mutual recognition of their respective quests.

"I think we could arrange that," Althea finally responded, a cryptic smile floating on her lips. "Sharing the road with companions could prove to be... enriching."

The pact was sealed with handshakes and nods of agreement. Althea, Diane, and Iris, each bearing their own burden of stories and secrets, prepared to embark on the next chapter of their journey together, united by the prospect of a future where their destinies would be inextricably linked.

❖ ❖ ❖

CHAPTER 6: THE CHALLENGE

The Ambush

The sun had just crossed the horizon when the three companions, Iris, Diane, and Althea, left Valdor to begin their journey along the Azure Lake. The path was caressed by a gentle breeze that made the tall grass dance, and the clear blue sky was marked only by the lazy passage of a few solitary clouds.

The lake, like a gigantic sapphire jewel, sparkled under the morning rays, reflecting the majesty of the southern mountains. Its calm waters were bordered by smooth pebbles and fine sand, where footprints told stories of the travelers before them. At times, they stopped to watch the silver reflections of fish playing on the surface, a peaceful spectacle inviting them to daydream.

To the north, the Tianzi Mountains stood, majestic and wild. Their silhouette cut through the sky, drawing gazes with their unaltered beauty and promise of adventures. The air there was crisper, laden with the sharp scent of conifers and the fragrance of high-altitude flowers, an intoxicating mix that awakened the senses.

Iris walked with a feline grace, her eyes scanning the distance as if she could read the shadows of the past and the whispers of the wind. Diane, with her regal posture, moved with natural elegance, her golden hair catching the daylight like a halo. Althea, wrapped in her starry azure cloak, radiated a mystical calm, the serenity of her mage's spirit spreading around her like a soothing aura.

Their conversation was a harmonious mix of light laughter, whispered confidences, and knowing silences. They shared stories from their previous lives, weaving deeper connections with each step, with each exchange. Their differences, far from dividing them, enriched their journey, each bringing her unique color to the canvas of their union.

As the sun climbed high in the sky, their path led them to the edge of the steppes. The landscape opened onto a vast expanse of grass stretching as far as the eye could see, a turquoise ocean where the wind created waves of grass rippling in unison. It was a world apart, where time seemed suspended, inviting the travelers to exploration and discovery.

In this haven of tranquility, an unforeseen event was about to unfold, one that would test their nascent alliance and their courage. For the moment, they walked carefree, bathed in light and freedom, unaware of the shadow looming on the horizon.

As the trio cautiously advanced across the vast steppes, an unexpected chill swept through the air. The area, known to be a haven for brigands and outlaws, echoed with a silence too heavy to be innocent. The brilliantly blue sky suddenly darkened, as if the heavens themselves were bracing for imminent drama.

Iris, whose senses were honed by a life of assassination, sensed danger and suggested they quicken their pace. Her suggestion was barely uttered when a distant gleam betrayed the presence of their enemies. Before the threat was fully realized, Iris moved with the agility of a panther, intercepting a deadly arrow aimed at Althea. Her hand grabbed the shaft of the arrow, and her gaze hardened at the sight of the crystal tip – a mage-killer arrow.

With Iris's quick reflexes, the group was now fully alert to the danger. They quickly formed a defensive stance, ready to face the hidden assailants who had dared to attack them in this seemingly peaceful expanse. The adventure, which had begun with the promise of discovery and camaraderie, was now taking a turn into the treacherous realms of confrontation and survival.

The realization struck like a clap of thunder: someone had deliberately planned an attack against the mage of their trio. Iris, scanning the horizons, warned her companions. Diane, whose nobility was matched only by her courage, stood ready to fight, while Althea, her face marked by determination, erected a protective dome around them, a shimmering energy barrier against the darkness assailing them.

Time seemed to stretch, each second an eternity, as Iris leaped towards the source of the shots. Althea, channeling her powers, spoke through the winds to warn Iris of the potential for additional magical threats among their attackers.

The battle was brief but intense. Upon her return, Iris was wounded, but her training had conferred resilience against poisons that would have felled anyone else. However, the victory was short-lived. Diane, the carefree princess with an ever-bright smile, lay with a poisoned arrow lodged in her leg.

Althea immediately sprang into action, her hands glowing with a soft light as she attempted to neutralize the poison. Iris, panting from the skirmish, kept watch, ensuring that no further threats approached. Diane, despite the pain, managed a weak smile, her spirit unbroken even in the face of danger. The trio, bound by their shared ordeal, now faced a new challenge: to heal and protect one of their own, deepening their bond and determination to reach Seranthea safely.

Panic was a looming threat. Iris, the usually unflappable warrior, faltered at the sight of a weakened Diane. The pain of the wound paled in comparison to the anguish in Diane's eyes. "It's nothing," she tried to reassure, despite the fever already painting her cheeks with a deceptive flush.

Althea, with all the concentration her art demanded, busied herself with slowing the poison. Her incantations, gentle and rhythmic, wove a protective weave around the wound, halting the progress of the poison threatening Diane's life.

"Poison?" Diane's voice was a thin thread, vibrating with fear despite her bravery.

Iris, with a tenderness no one would have suspected, placed a hand on her shoulder, promising healing. "Mages have remedies for everything, right, Althea?" she asked, searching the mage's eyes for a glimmer of hope.

Althea nodded, magic blossoming from her fingertips like petals in the wind. "We'll reach the Sanctuary of Solis. The healers there will help us." The determination in her voice was a beacon in the storm, a solid anchor to cling to.

Together, they carefully lifted Diane, preparing to

make haste towards the sanctuary. Each step was a testament to their unity and resolve, their journey now taking on a new urgency - not just a quest for answers, but a race to save one of their own.

The journey to the Sanctuary of Solis was a test of will. Every step was an act of faith, each breath a silent prayer. They supported Diane, their precious burden, through golden meadows and winds singing ancient hymns.

The colors of twilight mingled with their elongated shadows, painting a fresco of their determination. The setting sun set the sky ablaze, its fire reflecting in Iris's steely gaze, in Diane's golden hair, and in Althea's aura, uniting their silhouettes in a dramatic tableau of survival and solidarity.

The Sanctuary of Solis was only a day's march away, but each minute was a battle against time, a struggle for life. In this fight, they were one, three souls bound by fate, walking together towards the light of an uncertain dawn.

The scene was imbued with a poignant mix of despair and determination. Althea and Iris, stepping away from Diane's earshot, confronted the thorny truth of their situation.

Althea whispered, "Her condition is worsening. We need to make it to the sanctuary by tomorrow's dawn, or I fear the worst."

Iris nodded grimly, her eyes scanning the horizon for the shortest path. "Then we'll travel through the night if we must," she declared, her voice resolute.

Their resolve was clear: they would face the night, the exhaustion, and the uncertainty, for the life of their friend and companion hung in the balance.

Iris, her expression hardened, listened to Althea's confession, her skepticism momentarily giving way to understanding. "So, it's a vendetta you've dragged us into," she said, her voice a mix of frustration and concern.

Althea nodded, her gaze heavy with guilt. "Yes, and it's why I can't continue with you after we reach the sanctuary. I refuse to endanger you and Diane any further."

Iris looked away, her thoughts racing. "We're in this together now, Althea. You can't just walk away because the road gets hard."

Althea's shoulders slumped, a visible sign of her internal struggle. "Iris, my journey with you was meant to be a brief one. I never intended to involve you in my troubles. But I promise, I'll do everything in my power to ensure Diane's recovery and your safety."

The conversation ended with a tense silence. Despite the rift, their immediate concern was Diane's well-being. They resumed their journey, the weight of Althea's revelation adding a somber tone to their steps. The night ahead was long, and the path to the Sanctuary of Solis, though illuminated by the promise of healing, was now shadowed by the complexities of their intertwined fates.

Iris's reaction was a blaze of cold fury and sharp disappointment. The words exchanged between them were cutting blades, each phrase revealing wounds deeper than physical injuries. The revelation that Althea had inadvertently played a role in the attack had led them to a crossroads of conflicting emotions.

Iris, her eyes filled with anger, clenched her fists. "And it hadn't occurred to you to warn us of this risk? Forewarned, they would never have taken me by surprise."

"It's what I'm saying, it's all my fault. I was caught up in this journey, and it was my first journey that I wasn't making alone..." Althea let her sentence hang, overwhelmed by guilt.

Iris sighed, a glimmer of understanding in her eyes: "That, I can understand. Then stay. For Diane. She seemed so happy to have a mage in our group; it felt like a band of adventurers on a world-changing quest."

"Exactly... I might be on a quest of that magnitude. But she - Diane - has no place in this adventure; it's far too dangerous," Althea replied, her gaze drifting into the distance.

A branch snapped, interrupting them, and they turned to see Diane, listening with tears streaming down her cheeks.

"For you, I'm just a burden, just a defenseless noble who's capable of nothing. I don't have your magic, Althea, and I don't have your combat skills, Iris, but I know how to handle a bow, I have knowledge of alchemy, and I am an exceptional diplomat. But of course, you only see the blonde-haired princess."

Iris and Althea, taken aback, began, "Diane…"

Swallowing her tears, Diane continued forcefully: "Leave me, it's over. I'll go alone. To free my kingdom from the nascent grip of evil." She turned her back and began to walk, laboriously, then collapsed, harshly caught by the reality of her condition.

Without a word, Iris and Althea rushed to her. In that moment, the bonds of their sisterhood were strengthened, transcended by urgency and genuine affection. They lifted Diane, united by a silent promise to stay together, no matter the trials ahead. The steppe, under the twilight, became the witness to their tacit oath, their commitment to brave together the storms of their destiny.

❦ ❦ ❦

The Sanctuary

The Sanctuary of Solis rose majestically before them, a silhouette of stone and hope set against the twilight sky. The marble columns soared towards the heavens, seeming to strive to support the starry vault itself. Diane, weakened, rested in their arms, her feeble breathing setting the rhythm of their hurried steps.

Iris, her face caressed by the last rays of the setting sun, turned to Althea, her eyes filled with suspicion. "Who are you, really? You present yourself as an eternal student, but your knowledge seems to go beyond mere curiosity."

Althea responded with a gentleness tinged with unspoken truth, "I am an eternal student at heart, always aware of the extent of my ignorance."

Iris, with a hint of impatience, continued, "During the attack, when I asked for Diane's protection, you conjured a protective dome instantly, without incantations, and it was tinged with red – a hallmark of war magic."

Althea, her face darkening slightly, nodded. "You are indeed more observant than you appear. That's to your credit. War magic or not, it remains a defensive spell."

"One must be trained at the mage's war academy to master such magic," Iris left her sentence hanging, her eyes expressing a mix of curiosity and mistrust. "We all have our secrets, but don't let yours become a burden to Diane."

Althea, with a veil of melancholy in her voice, murmured, "Vigilance is essential, but knowing how to trust is just as important. Perhaps fate has brought us together for a reason we will discover in time. It is still too early to reveal certain secrets." She abruptly stopped, her gaze shifting towards three priestesses of the sanctuary who were approaching hastily.

One of the priestesses, short of breath, inquired about the situation. "Traveler, we are going to assist your friend. Any information useful for the care?"

Althea quickly explained her magical intervention while Iris described the nature of the poison with a precision that would not have been out of place in the archives of a master assassin.

Impressed despite herself, Althea observed, "Expert in poisons."

Then, addressing the priestess, she added, "Can you tell Mirela Moonsong that Althea is here?"

The priestesses hurried to transport Diane inside, leaving Iris and Althea alone on the cold steps of the sanctuary. They sat down, two weary silhouettes seeking a moment of respite.

The sanctuary was a place out of time, where the marble seemed to absorb the world's sufferings. The engravings on the walls told stories of heroism and healing, while the wind carried the whispers of the faithful in prayer. It was a world of fragile peace, a sanctuary in the purest sense of the word.

Althea and Iris, exhausted from the day's trials, succumbed to the serenity of the place. The weight of revelations and shared secrets seemed to lighten a bit, eclipsed by the hope that Diane would soon be out of danger. Twilight draped its veil over the sanctuary, and in this holy place, even the darkest truths could be approached with hope and trust.

Thus they waited, two warriors bound by fate, heads full of tumultuous thoughts and hearts heavy with hope, watching the last glows of the day fade and the stars take their place in the firmament. The Sanctuary of Solis, bathed in soft and comforting light, offered them a haven, a moment of calm before the storm that was sure to return with the dawn.

CHAPTER 7: CROSSED DESTINIES

The Priestess Of The Silver Moon

Twenty-eight years ago, in the dark and silent streets of Valoria, under the silver light of the full moon and the veil of a pouring rain, a scene of immeasurable desolation unfolded. Valerius, the aspiring archmage, ran with desperate urgency, leaping over obstacles, guided by a foreboding premonition. The moonlight and the relentless rain hindered his run, but Eliora's abode was in sight. Two shadows fled from the house, one carrying what seemed to be a child. "I'm too late," he thought, torn between pursuing the shadows and his concern for Eliora.

He entered the dwelling, his heart heavy with fear. There, Eliora lay on the ground, life escaping from her body like the last drops of a summer rain. Valerius rushed to her side, desperately trying to administer magical aid. "Eliora, answer me!" he implored, but his efforts were in vain.

With a final breath, she whispered weakly, "They took her... my little one...". The pain in her eyes was a mirror to Valerius's soul, shattered by sorrow.

"I will find her, I promise you, Eliora," he vowed,

tears mingling their salt with that of the beating rain.

Eliora breathed her last, taking with her a part of the light that brightened Valerius's life. The house, once a haven of peace, transformed into a transient mausoleum, a silent testament to the tragedy that had just unfolded. The heavens wept, the torrential rain seeming to want to wash away the scene of the crime, but nothing could erase the unforgivable act that had occurred.

Overwhelmed by a whirlwind of grief and guilt, Valerius collected himself, remembering Eliora's last words. He hurried upstairs, where he found Mirela, Eliora's daughter, hidden in a closet. She was wrapped in sheets, her innocent gaze tragically contrasting with the brutality of the situation. Valerius took the young girl into his arms, determined to protect her at all costs.

The next day, as the first light of dawn pierced the grieving sky, Valerius crossed the gates of the Sanctuary of Solis. The archpriestess, a woman of infinite wisdom and compassion, welcomed him with maternal gentleness. "I entrust this child to you," declared Valerius, his voice rough with emotion. "Her mother was a friend, a light in our world, now extinguished. Protect her, raise her in peace and in the love of these sacred walls. Her name is Mirela, Mirela Moonsong."

The high priestess accepted the charge with a silent promise, an unspoken oath of protection and love. "What a beautiful name. She will be cherished and loved here, as my own daughter," she replied, her eyes shining with a glimmer of hope and determination.

So ended a tragic chapter in Valerius's life, a memory that would forever be etched in his heart, a burden of sorrow and responsibility. But from this dark night, a new dawn was born, promising a better future for little Mirela, the last vestige of Eliora's love and light.

And thus, Mirela was christened the Priestess of the Silver Moon, a child of prophecy and promise, growing under the guidance of the sanctuary's priestesses. She learned to know peace, to sing harmony, and to heal with a grace unique to her. Her prayers rose, and her hands, bathed in light, wove webs of healing over wounded bodies and souls. Her voice became the echo of hope, and her presence, a beacon in life's storms.

Yet, despite the tranquility surrounding Mirela, the mystery of her past remained, a veiled shadow pulsating in her heart.

Mirela Moonsong, the Priestess of the Silver Moon, continued to walk her path of light, unaware of the truth hidden in the folds of her story. For truth is often like the moon, revealing an illuminated face while leaving the other in shadow, waiting for time to unveil the buried secrets.

* * *

The Guardian Of The Forgotten Arcana

There are moments in the history of Elysorium when fate takes an unexpected turn, weaving threads that connect souls in a manner as mysterious as it is significant. The story begins thus, with a messenger hawk and a request of the utmost importance.

Three years after the assassination of Eliora, Valerius, newly appointed as archmage, received a message from the high priestess of the Sanctuary of Solis. The content was brief but imperative, urging Valerius to immediately travel to the sanctuary. His heartbeats echoed with the anxiety of a protector, fearing for the safety of Mirela, Eliora's daughter, whom he had sworn to take care of.

Upon his arrival, the high priestess reassured him: Mirela, now three years old, was in perfect health. But the purpose of the invitation was of a different nature. The priestess led Valerius to the nursery, where a crib housed a sleeping little girl, as peaceful as she was mysterious. "I ask you to take this child to the Seranthea orphanage and to take her under your protection," the priestess declared in a voice imbued with unusual solemnity.

Valerius, taken aback, asked for explanations. Who was this child? Why was she abandoned? But the priestess merely told him that the child's mother had entrusted her to the sanctuary and that, for everyone's good, it was better that he remain ignorant of her lineage. Thus, with a heart heavy with unanswered questions, Valerius took the little girl to the Seranthea orphanage, unaware that this act would mark the beginning of an extraordinary saga.

She grew up in the orphanage, quickly proving herself to be an exceptional student. Her intelligence, thirst for knowledge, and innate affinity with the crystals of the Seranthea plains earned her the nickname 'the crystal mage'. But it was under the title of 'little prodigy' that she was most often recognized, whether in admiration or jealous sarcasm. Her exceptional abilities in the study of ancient and foreign magic attracted the attention of the most eminent mages of the era.

Regarded as a prodigy by all her masters, she became a guardian at a remarkably young age, the youngest in the history of Elysorium. The role of the guardian is shrouded in mystery; these exceptional individuals are chosen for their unparalleled scholarship and unwavering will.

They are the guardians of forbidden arcana, spells so powerful and dangerous that their very existence must be concealed. Legend has it that the forbidden library - accessible only to the guardians - descends into the bowels of the earth, housing ancient magics, banned elvish spells, demonic incantations, and many other unfathomable secrets.

With her stellar intelligence and unfathomable soul, she was destined for this role. She embodied the perfect guardian, capable of resisting the seductive call of the absolute power represented by this forbidden knowledge. In the depths of the library, where the grimoires and scrolls seemed to live of their own will, she was also condemned to solitude.

Althea's rise was not just a triumph of intelligence and determination; it was also a burden, that of bearing the darkest secrets of Elysorium. In the silent corridors of the library, she moved like a shadow among shadows, a presence as elusive as the mysteries she guarded. Her solitude was not that of physical isolation, but that of a soul bearing the weight of the world on its shoulders, a guardian watching over the darkness so that the light may continue to shine.

Thus, in the pages of Elysorium's history, Althea emerged as a solitary star in the night, a dancing light in the heart of an abyssal universe. Her journey, from the orphanage to the sacred halls of the forbidden library, was an odyssey of knowledge, a voyage through the soul of a guardian of forgotten arcana.

CHAPTER 8: THE GOLDEN FURY

The Golden Fury

In the warmth of the night, under a veil of twinkling stars, the silhouettes of Iris and Althea were outlined, sitting on the cold stone in front of the Sanctuary of Solis. The silence was almost total, except for the wind whispering through the ancient colonnades, carrying with it the prayers and hopes of the faithful.

Iris's voice broke the night's calm, tinged with guilt and resolution, her words falling heavily in the air like stones in the calm water of a lake. "If she doesn't fully recover, I could never forgive myself. If I can't protect her from mere bandits... What will happen in Naragath..."

Althea, with a voice wise and tempered by knowledge of the mysteries and the dangers of the world, replied, "So you really want to go and face the necromancer on his land... Assassin, but no less naive than a princess. Do you know what awaits you if you manage to get past Lunaris? Are you familiar with that desert?"

Iris's determination did not falter in her eyes. "No.

But it doesn't matter, I'd rather die than give up. And then… the princess… I think I've found a reason to live."

"To get killed, rather than to kill, is that it? I'll help you to Seranthea. Valerius will make you see reason, and maybe he'll have your answers."

Iris was about to reply when suddenly, a radiant glow burst from Althea's pendant. A reddish magic dome unfolded around her, turning night into day with a blinding light. A thunderous voice, seeming to descend from the heavens themselves, resounded, "DIVINE PUNISHMENT!"

The impact struck the magic dome with unimaginable power, causing the sanctuary to tremble and debris to fall from the sacred columns. The dome cracked, just like Althea's pendant, which also fissured under the force of the assault.

Althea, lost, murmured, "Who… why…" while Iris, disoriented by the sonic impact, regained her senses.

Before them, a figure emerged through the blinding light, enveloped in an aura of divine power. She slowly raised her arms, as if drawing her energy from the depths of the earth and the heavens, and began her incantation, her voice blending with the wind and the energy surrounding her, "BY THE GLARE OF A THOUSAND SUNS…"

"STOP," intervened an authoritative voice. The high priestess appeared on the threshold of the sanctuary, imposing the "Sacred Sanctuary" seal. The light vanished as if by magic, and with it, Althea's protective dome. The high priestesses had the power to invoke the sanctuary spell, which prevents any magic within a radius around the holy place.

"Who dares disrespect this divine sanctuary?" challenged the high priestess.

The luminous figure, clad in shimmering golden armor, stepped forward, a radiant sword in her hand. "No sanctuary is above the judgment of God," she proclaimed, raising her sword for "DIVINE INTERVENTION." The priestess shuddered, aware of the imminent danger.

And at that moment, everything changed. "Celestia, stop!" The voice, weak but commanding, was that of Diane, supported by another priestess.

The stranger, Celestia, knelt deferentially, "My princess. Your captors owe you this moment of respite. They will pay for the tortures they have inflicted upon you." Her trembling voice betrayed her emotion, a tear running down her cheek.

Diane, with unexpected clarity, replied, "Celestia, these are not my enemies, but my saviors. I believe we need to clarify things..."

In the confusion of roles and intentions, a misunderstanding was dispelled, giving way to new hope. This scene, charged with raw emotion and revelations, would be etched in the legend of the Sanctuary of Solis as the moment when truth triumphed by the thread of a suspended sword.

✷ ✷ ✷

Introductions

In the comforting warmth of the room where the priestesses were dining, an attentive silence had settled, all eyes converging on Diane, who stood with unshakeable grace despite the fatigue marking her features.

"I introduce to you Celestia Seraphin, one of the twelve celestial paladins, sometimes known as 'The Divine Fury', I think you can see why."

The atmosphere was tinged with tension and astonishment, but Iris couldn't help but interject, a hint of irony in her voice, "I can confirm, I've never seen such blind fury!"

Celestia, whose golden armor reflected the light of the torches like many captured little suns, responded with a conviction that seemed unshakeable: "The blind are those who do not look directly at the light of God and–"

But she was interrupted by Althea, whose curiosity drove her to understand rather than to judge, "And why attack us?!"

Diane, with the wisdom of a born leader, took control of the conversation: "Celestia is my protector."

"It is my sole mission," confirmed Celestia, her voice as firm as the gleam of her sword.

"Celestia was deemed uncontrollable, impulsive, and rebellious by the other celestial paladins..." Diane let the sentence hang, looking at her protector with a mix of respect and affection.

Celestia attempted to protest, but Diane continued, "And so, she dedicates herself to my protection and must have thought you were my captors."

The story then unfolded, with Diane sharing with Celestia the trials and encounters that had marked their adventure so far. Celestia's eyes lit up with intense emotion, "A necromancer is after your mother. I can finally see my destiny, so many years of glimpsing it, now I know it."

Iris, not without a hint of humor, whispered to Althea, "I've never seen such an enlightened one, even too enlightened for other paladins!"

"The power of paladins is directly linked to their faith and the intensity of their feelings," explained Althea, "which explains why she managed to crack the protective pendant. What fury!"

Then, addressing the assembly with a voice that carried the warmth of friendship, Althea introduced, "As we are making introductions, let me present to you Mirela Moonsong, a priestess of light and my friend."

The tension dissipated like mist under the morning sun. They all dined together, with laughter echoing between the ancient walls, turning the misunderstanding into an anecdote that, in time, would be recounted with a nostalgic smile and mutual admiration. Fate, capricious and elusive, had woven its threads in an unexpected way, uniting these souls in a narrative that would be sung by bards for centuries to come.

❊ ❊ ❊

On The Way To Seranthea

In the spray of the waking dawn, the group stood in front of the Sanctuary of Solis, where the first rays of the sun caressed the ancient marble, heralding an imminent departure to Seranthea. Diane, her health restored by Mirela's magic, wore a radiant smile, reflecting her gratitude.

"Mirela, won't you come with us? We'll need a healer in our group! Besides, I really like you! And you look just like Iris, you could be her sister!" she exclaimed, a contagious laughter escaping her lips.

These words triggered a ripple in Iris, an echo of the priestess's earlier words. "Let's set off, it's time to get answers to our questions," she declared, a determined glimmer shining in her steel eyes.

Mirela, humble and devoted, looked at the high priestess, her mentor and spiritual guide: "My place is at the sanctuary, by the side of the high priestess."

"However," interjected the high priestess, "you could accompany them to Seranthea. I do need some rare crystals and also a scroll that was to be sent to me by Archmage Valerius."

"Understood, mother," Mirela replied with respect tinged with affection.

Their convoy, consisting of Mirela, Iris, Diane, Althea, and Celestia, set off for the city of mages. They left the shimmering shores of Lake Blanc, leaving behind the Sanctuary of Solis, and headed south, light-hearted, walking on the path that snakes between the Forest of the Four Winds and the Marshes of Whispers.

The road unfolded before them like a promise, an invitation to adventure, lined with the melody of the marshes' whispers and the rustling of leaves in the trees. Diane shared her childhood memories with Iris, recalling sunsets over the Crystal Plains, moments of such pure beauty that they seemed to suspend time itself.

As they ventured onto the road, two hungry young wolves emerged, their glowing eyes reflecting intent and hunger. Celestia, her features marked by the rigor of a life devoted to battle, brandished her sword and began her invocation, "BY THE GLARE OF A THOUSAND SUNS..." But Iris, with agility and precision that spoke of her years of training, threw her daggers before Celestia could finish, ending the threat in an instant.

Althea, with a smirk, addressed Celestia, "I think we're going to have to start talking strategy. It seems to me that exploding a thousand suns is a bit excessive for two young wolves." A nod of agreement circulated among them, followed by unanimous laughter. Celestia, slightly sullen but with a glint of self-ridicule in her eyes, retorted, "Very well. But you can never be too careful with wolves..."

Their laughter was interrupted by awe at the view that unfolded before them. The Crystal Plains revealed themselves in all their splendor, a carpet of sparkling gems under the caress of the sun. In the distance, the city of Seranthea shimmered like a mirage, an oasis of light and knowledge. The crystals, like stars fallen to earth, refracted the light into a kaleidoscope of colors, painting a living canvas of light and magic.

Iris, her eyes wide with wonder, advanced cautiously, captivated by the shimmer of the crystals. "It's like walking in a dream," she murmured, her voice a mix of admiration and astonishment.

Diane, walking alongside her, smiled, immersed in childhood memories. "My mother used to bring me here, to watch the sunsets. Each crystal shone like a star, an unforgettable visual symphony," she shared, her voice tinged with nostalgia.

Celestia, moving with the dignity of a warrior, her glittering golden armor, looked like a living crystal among the crystals. Her reflection in the gems added to the magic of the moment, a celestial warrior among the terrestrial stars.

Mirela and Althea, familiar with these wonders, advanced with a sense of reverence. Althea, delighting in the emanations of magic, shared her knowledge, "Each crystal is a concentration of magical energy, a well of dormant knowledge."

However, her expression became more serious as she added, "It is best to stay on the periphery. The concentration of magic here can be overwhelming, even harmful to those not accustomed to such forces."

Guided by Althea, they proceeded cautiously, skirting the edges of the Crystal Plains, while remaining awestruck by their beauty and power. Each step was a balance between admiration and caution, a path tread between fascination and respect for the ancient forces slumbering beneath their feet.

Finally, after crossing this enchanting landscape, the city of Seranthea revealed itself to them, shimmering like a mirage, an oasis of light and knowledge. The crystals, like stars fallen to earth, refracted the light into a kaleidoscope of colors, painting a living canvas of light and magic.

Astonished, they entered the city, passing through the ornate gates that seemed to welcome truth-seekers and knowledge-keepers with equal benevolence. The streets of Seranthea bustled with scholarly activity, mages wandering between libraries and laboratories, while markets offered curious onlookers wonders and treasures from all corners of the known world.

Their journey through the city was a journey

through knowledge itself, each cobblestone, each building, telling the story of a people dedicated to the eternal quest for knowledge. The music of the spheres seemed to harmonize with their passage, and in the air floated the promise of secrets to be discovered and mysteries to be unraveled.

It was a city of crystallized dreams, of theories woven into the very fabric of reality, where each spoken word resonated with the weight of history and each thought was a spark in the darkness of ignorance. And for our travelers, Seranthea was more than just a stop on their quest – it was a reflection of what humanity could achieve with willpower, audacity, and a mind open to the wonders of the universe.

Their adventure was just beginning, but already, they knew that the bonds forged on the road, in trials and laughter, were those that would illuminate the darkest paths and guide their steps towards ever-broader horizons.

CHAPTER 9: THE CITY OF MAGES

Seranthea

Within Seranthea, the city of mages, the air vibrated with the echo of whispered spells and the light from crystals that dotted the celestial vaults. The very architecture seemed bent by the will of the arcanists, with towers and buildings soaring towards the heavens as if to capture the secrets of the gods.

Althea, her eyes sparkling with pride, led the way, guiding her companions through the enchanting metropolis. "Seranthea is not just a place, it's a song of hope and possibilities," she told them, her hands tracing the curves of the buildings as if she were sculpting them in the air.

The first stop was the Garden of Constellations, a botanical labyrinth where each path aligned with a constellation, the plants chosen for their nocturnal blooming reflecting the light of the corresponding stars. "At night, it's as if the sky descends among us," Althea murmured, "and everyone can walk among the stars."

Then they crossed the Bridge of Whispers, a translucent masterpiece suspended over the Murmur River. Here, winds were captured in crystal containers, each singing a different melody when the wind passed through, creating a natural symphony that accompanied the passersby.

They passed by the Endless Library, a labyrinth of knowledge said to extend as far underground as it soared high into the sky. The facades were engraved with ancient runes that illuminated upon the approach of seekers, guiding them to the works they sought.

Leaving behind the learned echoes of the Endless Library, with its runes whispering centuries of knowledge, their path gently led them to the junction between erudition and creation. As they moved away, the lights of the runes dimmed in their wake, as if to seal the secrets once shared. The transition from ancient knowledge to modern ingenuity was palpable, naturally leading to the Workshop of Horizons.

Within the sacred enclosure of Seranthea, the Workshop of Horizons emerged as a promise of infinity. This space, where aspiring mages and revered masters crossed paths, was a nexus of converging energies. Here, the walls were inlaid with gems that pulsed with the rhythm of the earth, and globes of light floated, guiding apprentices in their meditations. Althea, with a look of admiration in her eyes, led them among the worktables where mages wove the threads of the future, creating artifacts destined to become legendary. "Every creation here is the beginning of a new adventure," she explained to them, her voice a silver thread in the fabric of the studious silence.

Further on, they arrived at the Dome of a Thousand Truths, a sanctuary of divination where floating crystal orbs revealed fragments of the future to those who dared to question fate. Under the dome open to the sky, spheres twirled, emitting flashes of light that cast passing visions onto the marble walls, offering glimpses of the potentialities of tomorrow. "Mages come here seeking guidance, but the wisest know that each vision is just one thread among a tapestry of possibilities," Althea whispered, guiding their steps through the kaleidoscope of the future.

Their exploration of Seranthea was a journey through embodied magic, each street corner, each cobblestone, each breeze laden with a story and a spell. It was a city where the ordinary mingled with the extraordinary, where each day was a celebration of the ancient art of mages and a hymn to the infinite potential of the human soul.

Finally, they headed towards the Tower of Archmage Valerius. The tower itself was a spiral of stone and glass, coiling like the shell of an ancient celestial gastropod. It pulsed with magic, its shimmering walls reflecting the different schools of magic taught within.

At the entrance, a gargoyle composed of ancient stones and protective glyphs, greeted them with a voice that seemed made of thousands of overlapping whispers. "Welcome, truthseekers," it said, stepping aside to let them enter.

Inside, the tower was even more impressive. Spiraling staircases floated without support, ascending and descending between floors as if carried by an invisible will. Globes of light, resembling captured fireflies, illuminated the path, and the air was imbued with the scent of magical ink and old parchments.

Althea led the group through the silent corridors, each step echoing on the marble like a heartbeat in the chest of the world. "Archmage Valerius is the guardian of knowledge, the bridge between the old and the new," she explained. "He is the one who will help us understand the mysteries that surround us."

❋ ❋ ❋

The Disappearance

As the group ascended the ethereal spiral of Archmage Valerius's Tower, their hearts beat with anticipation and anxiety, intermingling like the colors of an uncertain twilight. The tower, like a guardian of ancient mysteries, seemed to vibrate with the hidden whispers of long-gone mages, its presence a canvas stretched between the past and the future.

At the top, they were greeted not by the Archmage, but by his disciples, their faces etched with anxiety. "Mistress Althea," one of them began, his voice trembling, "Archmage Valerius has been missing since his last journey, and his echoes have been silent for several days." The weight of Valerius's absence fell upon them, heavy as the veil of the falling night.

Then, a mage handed Althea a series of messages left by the messenger falcon. Althea unrolled the messages delicately, as if she feared the words might fly away. The message from Valerius, written in a firm and familiar hand, vibrated with optimism that now seemed a distant murmur: *"I am in Solaria, all is well. I have visited Hestia Carmina, she hopes to see Althea soon!"* The familiar and warm tone of Valerius brought a slight comfort. The mention of Hestia Carmina, a renowned figure among the sages, drew a fleeting smile on Althea's lips, who murmured, "Hestia, guardian of the eternal flames..."

The last message was more concerning: *"Tomorrow, at sunrise, I leave for Lunaris. The situation is alarming, the city is closed to mages. It's inexplicable. Cassandra should welcome me."* Althea repeated the name Cassandra like an incantation, a keystone in the arch of their quest.

The disappearance of Valerius cast a shadow of uncertainty over their quest. Althea, hesitant to meet the gaze of her companions, remained silent.

The disciples clarified that no action had been taken, as no sign of danger had been detected. The mages indeed had spells and artifacts capable of signaling any critical situation or imminent danger, suggesting that Valerius might be safe.

But for now, they found themselves in the learned city of Seranthea, where each element held an ancestral lesson. They had to take advantage of this time to prepare, gathering strength and wisdom in anticipation of the challenges ahead. In their quest for truth, every clue was precious, weaving their destiny into the vast tapestry of history.

And as the stars began to sprinkle the emerging twilight, they knew that their adventure was far from over. The disappearance of Valerius was yet another mystery to unravel, a shadow to be chased away by the light of their perseverance. With the tower as their silent witness, they vowed to follow the path of answers, regardless of the winds and tides that fate had in store for them.

✤ ✤ ✤

The Strategy

In the heart of the library of the Tower of Mages, the whispers of ancient scrolls mingled with the voices of these five adventurers. Althea stood, embodying resolution and intellect, her shadow of wisdom tempered by the worry that veiled her gaze. "The lack of news from Valerius is unusual... There must be a reason," she pronounced, infusing her words with as much comfort as hope, as much for herself as for her companions.

"Take advantage of the bustle of Seranthea, regain your strength," she advised, her voice revealing a slight anxiety. "Let's meet this evening at the Dancing Mage Inn. I need to organize our departure for Solaria and contact Iridia Skyfury at Stellarae. She must be informed."

Her eyes scanned the horizon, as if she could decipher the mystery surrounding Valerius. "Once we cross the strait, we will be entering hostile territory...."

As night fell over Seranthea, it draped the city in a mystical aura. The alleyways lit up with laughter and whispers, the night stalls sparkling under candlelight. Mages, free from their daytime duties, animated the streets with their tales and enchantments. Despite the shadow hanging over their minds, the group allowed themselves to be captivated by the city's enchantment.

Under the protective shadow of the night, the Dancing Mage Inn welcomed them into its warm embrace. Around a hearty meal, Althea, emanating a natural leader's aura, shared her plan. "Iris and I will leave tonight, traveling light and fast, towards Solaria."

Celestia stood up, her gesture resonating with silent determination. Althea's presence never ceased to amaze her.

Iris, attentive, inquired about the route to take. "The Eastern Shield or the acid marshes. A tough choice, but necessary for speed," Althea explained, her eyes sparkling with strategy.

Turning to the rest of the group, she continued: "Celestia, Mirela, Diane, you will leave with the caravans tomorrow. A desert expert will accompany you. In Solaria, Ruby Foxglove will contact you. In case of danger, Hestia Carmina will offer you refuge."

Iris, impressed despite herself, observed Althea. How could she, so young, exude so much presence and skill? It was as if the mage had lived a thousand lives, each adding to her aura of command.

The Eastern Shield mountains were known for their inhospitality, and the climate was harsh enough to freeze bones. "Equip yourselves well. When you arrive, I hope Iris and I will already have some answers..."

Iris, her eyes twinkling with unwavering humor, added, "Here we go, a journey with the novice student mage who wields war magic like I wield a dagger." Her wink at Althea triggered a round of companionable laughter around the table.

Althea, though young, commanded respect with her charismatic aura. She possessed that indefinable quality of born leaders, those who naturally emerge in times of crisis, ready to guide others through the darkest storms.

Thus, the group split into two, separate strands of the same will, divided by the path but united by a common goal. In the warmth of the inn, plans were refined, final words were exchanged with gravity, and hearts were bound by a friendship forged in the trial and fire of battles to come.

Their parting was not a goodbye, but a tacit promise to reunite, enriched with new knowledge and ready to face together the challenges that awaited them. For in the dance of fate, every step apart was merely a prelude to a future gathering, where each experience would be shared and every victory celebrated with the fervor of those who have journeyed through shadows to reach the light.

CHAPTER 10: THE CITY OF THE SUN

Departure To Solara

In the enveloping softness of the night, under the brilliance of the stars that seemed to guide their way, Iris and Althea left the city of mages, Seranthea, through the Zenith Gate. Their departure, discreet and swift, was marked by a budding complicity, a harmony of steps and intentions resonating in the silence of the night.

Their earlier visit to Althea's home had revealed a living space steeped in solitude and knowledge. Shelves laden with books, ancient grimoires, and scrolls dotted the space, each object telling a story, each page whispering a secret. Iris observed, slightly fascinated, this cave of Althea's, a reflection of her mind as vast as distant galaxies.

Among the treasures in Althea's cave, a celestial globe particularly caught Iris's attention. Suspended in the air, it rotated slowly, casting constellations of light on the walls. The stars and planets, meticulously inlaid with precious stones, shimmered with a soft and mesmerizing glow. This globe was not just a work of art; it was a compendium of the universe, an atlas of the heavens that seems to pulse with its own life. "It's an inheritance from my master," explains Althea, following the graceful movement of the globe with her gaze. "Each gem represents a star, and each constellation has a story. It's a reminder that we are all connected to the grand ballet of the universe." Her voice took on a tone of nostalgia as she gently caressed the surface of the globe, as if to awaken memories of nights spent studying the mysteries of the stars.

Althea, in a whirlwind of preparations, handed various enchanted objects to Iris. "Take this, put it in your bag," she said, handing her a mysterious artifact. "Put on this necklace, wear this bracelet, keep this potion." Iris hardly had time to protest before she found herself adorned with sparkling jewelry, strangely contrasting with her assassin's attire. The diadem that Althea entrusted to her, a delicate work of metal and luminous stones, seemed to be the key to some unknown secret.

As they crossed the city gate, the world of Seranthea faded behind them, giving way to the vastness of the night and the mysteries it holds. The stars, like benevolent eyes, watched over their path, while the moon, a pale crescent in the sky, lit their way.

Their journey was more than a mere crossing; it was a dance between shadows and light, a silent ballet where each movement was measured, each gesture laden with meaning. The complicity between Iris and Althea, forged in the flames of past trials, shone in their eyes and reflected in their confident steps.

Their hearts beat in unison with the rhythm of the night, and their minds intertwined in a fabric of trust and determination. Together, they delved into the unknown, two souls bound by a fate that transcended them, two warriors walking side by side towards the answers that only the future could provide.

And in this night where time seemed suspended, their journey towards Solaria began, a promise of adventures yet to be written. In the enveloping serenity of the Valley of Tranquility, Iris and Althea, lulled by the whisper of leaves and the lapping of rivers, set up their camp. Under the starry night, they prepared for a few hours of rest before dawn would repaint the sky with its shimmering colors.

As they prepared to drift into sleep, Iris, a shadow of concern in her eyes, murmured, "I hope you chose the warrior accompanying them well, I can't help but worry."

Althea, with a reassuring smile on her lips, responded in a gentle voice, "With Celestia at their side, they are already safe on this part of the continent. But to ease your mind, I asked Ukrolm, known as 'The Colossus of Kethara', to accompany them."

At these words, a smile formed on Iris's lips. It was not just a smile of relief, but also one of admiration and gratitude for Althea's foresight. "You..." she whispered, a fleeting glint of tenderness lighting up her eyes.

Knowing Ukrolm's reputation well, Iris fell asleep peacefully, reassured by Althea's wise choice. In that suspended moment, under the starry sky, their hearts beat in unison, united in trust and hope for the challenges ahead.

As the first rays of the sun pierced the horizon, Iris and Althea were already busy folding their camp. While packing her things, Iris couldn't help but share her excitement, "I can't believe Ukrolm will be accompanying them. I'd give anything to see Diane's face! I've heard so many legends about him! They say he's ten feet tall and that he once fought a griffin with his bare hands!"

Althea, with an amused smile on her lips, replied, "People love to exaggerate the feats of their warriors! He must be about seven and a half feet , and if he had really fought a griffin with his bare hands, he would probably be less imposing today." Their shared laughter echoed in the morning air, filling the valley with their good cheer.

Continuing their journey through the Valley of Tranquility, they were carried by the serene ambiance of the place. True to its name, the valley offered a landscape where time seemed suspended: a gentle wind caressed the yellowing leaves of the trees, and the silence was so profound that one could hear the flutter of a butterfly's wings.

Suddenly, Iris, pointing south, exclaimed in wonder, "Have you seen the color of that forest?! Those purple trees are magnificent! Is it because of the crystals?"

But Althea's smile faded. "That's the forest of Calista, the domain of Calista Nyxaria, the solitary magician. It's best to ignore its existence. Let's continue."

As night fell, they set up camp at the edge of the Sea of Icarion, an enclosed body of water, guarded by the Strait that separated Solara from Lunaris. Ahead of them to the south lay Solara, their next destination after circumventing the Eastern Shield through the valley.

The Burning Marsh, with its sulfurous vapors and acidic flows, awaited them at dawn. Althea prepared a cloth with an alchemical solution that crystallized the acidic gasses into a protective envelope. "Cover your face, it will allow you to breathe almost normally."

She then placed a diadem on Iris's forehead, an incredibly delicate piece with a magical gem that shimmered in the darkness of the swamp. "This stone will guide us without losing sight of us," she explained.

Iris, touched by Althea's thoughtfulness, felt that the mage might have already untangled some threads of the mystery surrounding them. Her intelligence, like the stars above them, guided their way through the darkness of the unknown.

The crossing of the Burning Marsh was done in tense silence, broken only by the crunch of crystals forming on their makeshift masks. The atmosphere was an acidic bite, each breath a challenge to suffocation. At the edge of the marsh, they collapsed, exhausted, freeing their faces from the crystallized veils that had barely protected them from the corrosive vapors.

Near the reassuring waves of the Sea of Icarion, they shed their soiled clothes, hastily rinsing them in the salt water. The sea, in its infinite majesty, seemed to welcome them, washing away their sorrows and pains.

Althea, her eyes shining with genuine admiration, watched Iris, whose body, sculpted by the demands of her art, revealed uncommon strength and grace. "Your muscles tell the story of your battles, Iris," she said with a sincere smile. "Every contour testifies to an iron discipline and an unshakeable spirit."

Iris, in turn, couldn't help but admire Althea, whose intelligence was rivaled by the splendor of her form yielding to the waves. "It's not just in wisdom that you excel," she thought, the mage revealing a beauty equal to her sharp mind.

The sun, in its celestial ascent, dried their clothes laid out on the warm sand, while they relished fish that Iris's skill had extracted from the sea. The scene, bathed in the golden light of the afternoon, was breathtakingly beautiful, a moment of eternity captured between the azure of the sky and the gold of the sand.

Althea broke the comfortable and peaceful silence that had settled. "Today's journey wasn't long, but it was tough," she conceded with a contented sigh. "The good news is that we are in Maridora and the path to Solara will be gentle and kind to us."

The beach became their refuge for the night, under a strikingly clear starry sky. The murmur of the waves cradled them, the warmth of the sand served as their bed, and they fell asleep with the assurance that the worst was behind them and that the adventure, though perilous, had granted them an unforgettable moment of peace.

After a resolute walk under the clear sky of Maridora, Althea and Iris saw the golden silhouettes of Solara, the southern pearl, begin to appear on the horizon. The city, built in homage to the sun, was an ode to the celestial body, with each structure reflecting its light in a way that seemed to revive the celestial flame itself. The tall central tower, topped with a shimmering dome, rivaled the brightness of the daytime star, its radiance visible even from leagues around.

The city gates opened before them without any resistance, the guards offering distracted nods, accustomed to a constant flow of adventurers and travelers. The intense light of Solara enveloped everything, bathing the city in a comforting warmth and brilliant clarity.

Iris, her eyes squinting under the omnipresent brightness, couldn't help but admire the light and colorful clothing of the passersby, who moved with carefree ease through the lively streets. The city, famous for its fine sandy beaches and crystal-clear waters, attracted souls seeking rest or adventure, and many, charmed by its solar aura, chose to make their home there.

Palm trees proudly rose along the marble-paved avenues, their fronds gently swaying in the sea breeze. The sound of the waves mixed with the city's hustle and bustle, creating a relaxing melody that invited relaxation and contemplation.

The architecture of Solara highlighted reflective and light materials, from white marble veined with gold to dazzling mosaics that adorned the fountains and public squares. The buildings, with their clean and elegant lines, harmonized with the open spaces, offering captivating perspectives and constantly renewed plays of light at every glance.

As they crossed the city, Iris and Althea were struck by the festive atmosphere that seemed to reign perpetually, with markets overflowing with exotic fruits and sparkling jewelry, while musicians and street artists generously shared their art. Solara was a living painting, a perpetual celebration of life under the benevolent gaze of the sun.

❊ ❊ ❊

The Phoenix And The Fox

When Althea mentioned the upper city, the upscale neighborhoods, Iris felt the gap between the knowledge-paved streets of Seranthea and the impending luxury of Solara. "Are we visiting the famous... what's her name again? Lissia?" Iris inquired, her memories still muddled by the recent ordeals.

"Hestia Carmina, the incandescent archmage, the one who commands the flames," Althea corrected with a smile lit up with respect. "One day, I'll tell you the story of the one known as 'The Scarlet Phoenix'."

"Phoenix, huh... So she's a mage who manipulates fire..." Iris pondered, impressed despite herself by the flamboyant nickname.

Althea nodded, confirming not only Hestia's talent for pyromancy but also their appointment. "She should be waiting for us with Ruby, who will go to greet our friends upon their arrival."

"Ah yes, the little trickster," laughed Iris, a mischievous smile playing on her lips, as they approached a dazzling residence.

Before them, the house stood with dignity, its entrance door adorned with an inscription that captured their attention: *"In the fiery heart of the flame, lies the will to forge destinies."* The words, carved into the solid wood, seemed to vibrate with an inner force, as if the door itself was the threshold to a world governed by flames.

Pushing the door open, they were welcomed by a garden resembling a volcanic landscape, where heat-resistant plants and lava stone intermingled in a strange harmony. It was a piece of land where life clung tenaciously, a perfect preamble to meeting a mistress of fire.

They then crossed a large room with majestic columns, leading to an open archway offering a spectacular view of the sea. The azure expanse spread majestically before their eyes, its immensity reflecting the sky like a mirror of the gods. The sea breeze, imbued with salt and mystery, caressed their skin, inviting contemplation.

The balcony, overlooking this maritime panorama, would surely have inspired the most sublime verses from Baldair the Voyager, a bard whose fame extends across kingdoms. Every component of this scene seemed to chant a hymn to beauty and eternity. It was a living fresco where sky, sea, and land united in a harmonious symphony of hues and lights, a silent poem celebrating the majesty of creation.

In the doorway, the silhouettes of Hestia Carmina and Ruby Foxglove stood out with striking elegance, like a perfect conjunction between fire and shadow. Hestia, with her flaming red hair, rippled like the glows of a fiery twilight, while her sapphire eyes shone with a burning passion for magic. Her demeanor was that of a guardian of the eternal flames, a mage who had learned to dance with danger, her presence evoking the comforting warmth and indomitable light of fire.

Beside her, Ruby Foxglove, the Amber-eyed

Trickster, embodied cunning and agility, wrapped in the darkness of her black cloak. Her presence was like a living shadow, slipping among the whispers of the city, as elusive as the night wind. The mischief in her smile and the intelligence in her eyes echoed the burning charisma of Hestia, forming an unlikely alliance where light and darkness coexisted without consuming each other.

The meeting of Iris and Althea with these two illustrious characters was a spectacle of harmonious duality, uniting the fiery charm of the archmage and the shadowy cunning of the trickster. Together, they formed a living tableau where each color and shape told the story of a world where power and finesse were the keys to all mysteries.

※ ※ ※

From The Sun To The Moon

The whispers of the city had faded into the golden warmth of the evening, there were only four silhouettes left, savoring a wine from the City of the Sun. Ruby, the Trickster, was explaining the situation with unusual gravity. 'The wind has turned in Lunaris, and mages have become unwelcome shadows,' she explained, revealing a growing tension within the city of light.

Iris tilted her head, her tone filled with confusion and urgency. "But what could justify such hostility? And Valerius, could he have been swept away by this wave of hatred?"

The look in Hestia's eyes, dark as ashes after an intense fire, was lost in the flames of her past. "History seems to be repeating itself... Once, my exile from my native island was marked by similar accusations," her voice echoed a distant memory, "accused of bearing dragon's blood, I was treated as a demon."

Althea, with the serenity of a chess master before the game board, shared her supposition. "Perhaps it is the work of Sarthax and his black paladins."

Ruby, skepticism dancing in her amber eyes, questioned the solidity of this hypothesis. "Black paladins in Lunaris? My steps have led me to every corner of the city without crossing their shadow."

Althea, with a voice as clear as the waters of Solara's fountains, made the connection. "Sarthax, the ally of the necromancer, would like to see Naragath purged of its mages. And Cassandra, the queen, shows no sign of resistance. Do you find that normal?"

Ruby, her gaze darkening, nodded her head, the pieces of the puzzle fitting together in her mind.

"If the queen remains passive, she could well be manipulated or controlled," she suggested.

Althea, with furrowed brows in a sign of reflection, added with palpable gravity, "And if Cassandra is not who she seems to be? Or if, like Diane's mother, she is under the influence of a mind control spell?"

A heavy silence fell upon the table, the air vibrating with tangible concern at the mention of a mind control spell. Hestia Carmina, the fire mage with piercing eyes, grasped the magnitude of Althea's fears.

Iris's concern translated into a question hanging in the warm air. "What do you plan to do?"

Althea, with the determination of a captain facing the storm, replied. "Tomorrow, I will go to Lunaris to find Valerius."

Iris was not in agreement. "We will go," she insisted.

But Althea shook her head. "Stay here with Hestia and Ruby. If my fears are correct, the situation could be more dangerous than we imagine."

Hestia and Althea exchanged a look heavy with unspoken words, and Ruby, a silent observer, perceived the weight of the 'arrangements' made by the young mage.

Iris could not contain an emotion mixed with

admiration and challenge. "Althea, after everything you've anticipated, you must know that I won't let you face Lunaris alone. That explains the diadem you entrusted to me, doesn't it?" Her eyes betrayed an unwavering determination, reflecting her nature as a protector.

A smile of recognition and respect blossomed on Althea's lips. "Indeed, Iris, I had considered that possibility." Her gentle voice carried the nuances of a strategist watching her plan unfold as expected, and her smile, illuminated by the candlelight, was that of a mage who finds an equal in the art of courage.

Hestia stood up, her shadow cast on the walls like a warning. "If Valerius has suffered the slightest harm, I will cross this strait myself."

Eyes met, each pair understanding the gravity of the situation. Hestia Carmina's threat was not mere bravado; it was the oath of an embodied power ready to defend its allies.

Althea nodded solemnly, the light of the strategist in her eyes. "I know, and we will do everything to avoid that."

The ensuing silence was filled with a shared resolution, an unspoken pact sealed between the lines of destiny. In this pact, solidarity and their strength were the torch that would guide their steps through the darkness of the days ahead.

Led by Hestia, whose radiant presence carved a path through the corridors of the dwelling, Iris and Althea arrived in front of a door carved with ancient runes, promising well-deserved rest. The fire mage opened the door with a gesture of hospitality, revealing a welcoming room bathed in the warm tones of twilight.

The comfort of the room was immediate, with a large, inviting bed draped in fine fabrics and plush cushions seemingly waiting to envelop them after the rigors of their journey. A subtle scent of incense floated in the air, mingled with the woody fragrances of mahogany furniture. Open windows let in the night breeze, carrying with it the distant whispers of the sea and the discreet chirping of crickets.

Althea approached the window, observing for a moment the stars that had begun to twinkle in the sky, before turning back to Iris with a sigh of relief. "Tonight, we can afford a little peace," she said, a tired but satisfied smile curling her lips.

Iris, exhausted but grateful, nodded silently, her mind already lulled by the promise of restorative sleep. Together, they prepared to yield to the arms of Morpheus, each slipping into the depths of a well-deserved rest, confident that under Hestia's watch, no dream could be disturbed by the shadows of the outside world.

CHAPTER 11: THE ANGEL AND THE COLOSSUS

A New Departure

In the heart of Seranthea, as dawn still stretched its shadow over the cobblestone alleys, Diane, Mirela, and Celestia gathered in the common room of the inn for an early breakfast. The air was fresh, carrying the promises of a busy day ahead.

The innkeeper, greeting them with a smile, inquired about their plans. Diane, her voice still veiled by the mist of sleep, replied that they had an imminent appointment at the Zenith Gate.

"It's to the east of the city. If you cross the Place of the Seven Veils, you'll be there in time to see the sunrise," explained the innkeeper, while serving them an assortment of fresh fruits from the jungles of Silvaria, at Diane's request.

Celestia, without lingering on the conversation, simply nodded and followed Diane's example. Mirela, on the other hand, opted for a more frugal snack, a bowl of gruel garnished with seeds and a touch of Maridora honey, reflecting her ascetic habits.

The innkeeper, while filling their plates, spoke of the charms of Solara, a popular destination for its mild climate and golden beaches. He also mentioned, not without a hint of concern in his voice, the recent bandit attacks on the roads and the difficulty of crossing the Eastern Shield, the mountain range separating them from the Maridora region.

Diane, careful not to reveal the true reasons for their journey, lightly spoke of their desire to bask on the famous golden beaches. Celestia, clumsy in her candor, began to reveal more than necessary, but was quickly interrupted by Diane who, with a discreet nod, asked her to be silent.

Once the meal was hastily finished, they gathered their belongings and set off through the still sleepy streets of the city, heading east. Diane then expressed her impatience about meeting the mercenary recommended by Althea, hoping that he would live up to their expectations.

Mirela, with a gentle and confident voice, expressed her unwavering trust in Althea, highlighting the almost mystical infallibility of the mage. Diane, with a wry smile, countered that no one was immune to mistakes, not even a mage as prodigious.

Celestia, steadfast in her devotion, couldn't help

but praise Diane's perfection, eliciting an exchange of knowing glances between Mirela and the princess.

As the first light of dawn began to caress the city's rooftops, turning shadows into shades of purple and gold, they reached the Zénith Gate. The Place of the Seven Veils, crossed in the morning tranquility, gradually came to life, marking the beginning of a new chapter in their journey.

The merchant convoy displayed its eclectic collection of carts and pack animals in front of the majestic Zénith Gate, the junction point between the safety of Seranthea and the uncertainty of travel routes. The person in charge, a middle-aged man with keen eyes and a face weathered by the winds of commerce, approached decisively.

"You are Diane, I presume, and these are your companions?" he asked, sweeping his gaze over the young woman's noble stature and the peaceful aura of her friends.

Diane, with the ease of a princess accustomed to court protocols, nodded gracefully. "Exactly, we are ready."

The merchant, consulting a worn register, said, "I was informed that a warrior would join us for the escort. Do you have any news?"

Before Diane could respond, Mirela pointed to a

figure approaching them, silhouetted against the brilliant tableau of dawn. "That must be our man."

All eyes turned towards the newcomer. A gigantic form advanced, his cape billowing like the banner of a titan. The light of the dawn, finally triumphing over the night's shadow, gradually revealed the contours of the individual, an imposing mass, a presence that asserted itself with the certainty of the elements.

His voice, a rumble that seemed to emanate from the earth itself, echoed in the morning calm. "Ukrolm of Kethara, at your service. Althea sent me to ensure your protection to Solara."

Diane couldn't help but stare at the giant's hand, a true iron grip that could crush wood like straw. The warrior set down his bag with a dull thud, revealing the contents of his arsenal, including a war ax so massive that even the sturdiest of men would have struggled to wield it easily.

The official, his features drawn with sudden anxiety, nodded with a less assured voice. "Well, let's get going then." Regaining his composure, he directed the travelers to the last wagon. "Put your belongings there."

The three companions, along with the warrior, stowed their gear. When Ukrolm placed his own bag, the wagon sagged under the weight, its wheels slightly sinking into the city ground.

"We will travel as long as the daylight is with us. If you feel tired, you can rest for a while on a wagon, but don't overdo it," warned the merchant, casting a pointed look at Ukrolm, whose mere presence seemed to defy the laws of physics.

At his command, the caravan set off, leaving Seranthea in a symphony of wheels and whinnies. And as they moved away, the rising sun painted their journey in shades of gold and amber, opening the next chapter of their epic.

The first day of travel stretched out, as gentle as the wind's breath in the branches of the magical woods. The companions, in harmony with the natural melodies of the place, walked in silence, intoxicated by the peace of a sanctuary where even time seemed to have fallen asleep to listen to the hymns of the birds.

In the twilight, the merchant pointed to a distant forest, bathed in the last rays of sunlight that made its trees glow with bark as red as embers and leaves tinged with the brilliance of amethysts. A diaphanous mist emanated from it, veiling the mystery of a tower that stood like a sentinel at its heart.

"The forest of Calista," he announced in a voice tinged with both respect and fear, "we will pass to the south, away from its enchanted silence."

Diane expressed her regret, melancholy in her gaze: "It's sad to bypass such a natural wonder."

Ukrolm, the colossal man with measured steps, allowed himself to comment, his deep voice resonating like an echo from the depths of the earth, "Calista's domain. Even the gods bypass it." His statement was final, putting an end to any debate.

Later, when the sky adorned itself in its finest attire to greet the setting king, the group arrived at the Two Rivers inn. The place was a haven of welcome, promising rest and conviviality.

The inn's table, under the warm glow of candles, welcomed the travelers. The caravan leader, his face illuminated by the flickering light, explained the challenges of the next day. "We will begin the crossing of the mountains. It's a tough path, but the view is all the more rewarding."

At dawn, as the stars faded, giving way to the nascent blue of the dawn, the group stood, contemplating the Eastern Shield. The mountain range stood majestically, its peaks and valleys etched against the horizon like a map of a celestial kingdom.

The mountains spread before them, a fan of sleeping giants under a blanket of mist and greenery. Nature, in its divine architecture, had sculpted passages, lower passes, where men had dared to carve paths. This was where their road led them, towards the trails winding among the stone giants, where every step would be an ascent towards the sky.

They left the inn, their hearts vibrating to the rhythm of the earth, their minds turned towards the heights that awaited them, ready to face the steep trails of the Eastern Shield. It was a tableau worthy of the greatest epics, an ode to adventure where each silhouette stood out, proud and determined, ready to climb the rungs of destiny.

❋ ❋ ❋

An Epic Battle

In the golden spray of dusk, the caravan wound through the last meanders of a mysterious wood. The caravan leader, scanning the horizon, announced, "A clearing with a welcoming stream lies ahead. That's where we'll set up camp for the night." But his plan was thwarted by a fallen tree, a sleeping giant blocking their path.

Then, like shadows emerging from the void, a group of brigands appeared. The leader, pointing a crossbow with deadly precision at the travelers, proclaimed in a thunderous voice, "Let's make this quick and easy. Follow my instructions, and you'll keep your lives."

The head of the merchants, more accustomed to negotiation than confrontation, offered with feigned restraint, "We have only rations, but we're willing to share..."

But the tension was palpable, a taut thread ready to snap at any sudden move.

The brigand cut him off sharply, "SILENCE! Women and children, over there by the tree. And leave your weapons on the ground!"

In a suffocating silence, two figures advanced; from a distance, they might have been mistaken for a man and a child. But as they drew closer, the true nature of these two protagonists was revealed. Ukrolm, freed from his cloak, stood there, a titan among mortals, his muscles seemingly sculpted by the gods themselves. "Ukrolm of Kethara, at your service," he roared, a mountain in motion.

Beside him, Celestia, donning her golden helmet, which shone with the light of faith and the fervor of battle, shed a tear of divine zeal. "I was born for this day," she whispered, "Thank you Almighty God for this chance to prove my worth."

The brigand leader, his voice losing assurance, issued a final warning: "Stop or..." But his words were lost to the wind as the two warriors charged with the speed of a storm.

The ensuing carnage was a ballet of strength and faith, a dance where the colossus and the angel felled their foes in a symphony of chaos, a whirlwind of steel and light.
The brigands, panicked, sought refuge in the trees, a scene that would have brought a smile even to the darkest of bards.

As the night unfurled its starry veil, the travelers, gathered in the clearing, shared laughter and meals under the benevolent gaze of the constellations. The day's events, now mere anecdotes, echoed among the laughter. Who knows, perhaps in a distant future, bards will sing of the feats of the angel and the colossus, whose courage scattered the shadows and etched into the marble of history a battle where bravery rivaled absurdity, a tale where terror gave way to the hilarity of brigands perched in trees like frightened birds.

✲ ✲ ✲

The Pearl Of The South

In the tranquility of the passing days, the arduous

mountains gave way to the verdant plains and forests of Maridora. After the epic battle and three more days of trekking, the brave adventurers, Diane, Mirela, Celestia, and Ukrolm, arrived at the glittering gates of Solara, the southern pearl.

Passing through the guards' checks and the wagon inspections, they entered the bustling city. The streets of Solara came alive beneath their feet, curious glances from passersby fixing on the eclectic group. Mirela and Diane, draped in their cloaks for discretion, contrasted with Ukrolm's imposing stature and Celestia's radiant golden armor. Diane smiled, thinking their contact would soon spot them.

They found refuge on a tavern terrace, overlooking the sparkling sea. Diane, a light smile on her lips, exclaimed, "In this city, it's easy to forget our missions. It almost feels like a vacation!"

Ukrolm, as imposing as he was relaxed, retorted, "While waiting for news from Althea, we might as well enjoy the city."

The conversation shifted to Althea, and Diane queried, "You seem to know her well, Ukrolm. For how long, exactly?"

Ukrolm answered with a knowing air, "Oh, it's been many moons since our paths first crossed."

Mirela, ever enigmatic and reserved, added in a soft

but melancholic voice, "With Althea, it's different. Her mind is as vast as the ocean, and her solitude as deep as the abysses. She carries on her shoulders secrets heavier than mountains."

Intrigued, Diane pressed on, "Secrets? But she seems well surrounded, doesn't she?"

Mirela gently shook her head, "Being surrounded doesn't drive away the solitude of a guardian. There's a distance in her gaze, an echo of a life burdened with invisible weights."

Ukrolm, changing the tone with his jovial manner, exclaimed, "The life of a warrior is much simpler! Strike first, think later, right, Goldielocks?" He playfully placed his hand on Celestia's shoulder, causing the table to sway under the weight of his strength.

Celestia, slightly taken aback but amused, couldn't help but smile. In her warrior's heart, she knew that a good shield smashsometimes spoke louder than words.

Thus, in the warm atmosphere of the inn, with the stars sparkling above the sea of Solara, they shared a moment of relaxation, away from the worries and shadows of their quest. A precious moment, a bubble of lightness in the whirlwind of their destiny.

Under the cloak of a brilliant moon, the troop, tired

but satisfied with their day, chose to spend the night at the inn. The idea of resting in real beds after so many days of travel resonated like a sweet melody to their weary ears.

The next morning, as the first rays of the sun timidly slipped through the shutters, they gathered around a table for breakfast. Diane broke the silence. "If we don't hear from this Ruby by tonight, we'll go to meet the fire archmage."

Ukrolm, lost in thought, murmured with a hint of respect in his voice, "The Phoenix..." His gaze betrayed his admiration for the legendary mage.

As they were conversing, a figure approached their table and sat down unceremoniously. The unexpected arrival of this stranger left no room for doubt: Ruby Foxglove, the Trickster, had made her entrance. Her eyes, sparkling with mischief, scrutinized each of them with amused curiosity.

Without waiting to be questioned, Ruby spoke in a light tone, yet with unshakeable confidence, "Were you looking for me?" Her presence brought a touch of mystery and intrigue to their morning already filled with questions.

Thus, the long-awaited meeting with Ruby Foxglove promised to be the start of a new chapter in their adventure, an unpredictable spark in the vast universe of Elysorium.

… … …

CHAPTER 12: THE GRASP OF THE ABYSS

The City Of The Moon

In the nascent dawn of Solara, Iris and Althea, their faces softened by the day's first light, shared a silent breakfast with Hestia. Their minds were already turned towards Lunaris, the enigmatic city at the gates of Naragath, where danger and mystery intermingled like heat and desert sand.

Althea broke the silence, her voice as clear as the horizon awaiting them: "We leave for Lunaris this morning."

Hestia, whose gaze betrayed a maternal concern, softly replied, "Please be careful. Ruby will contact you in two days to ensure your well-being."

Althea, with the determination of a mage embracing her destiny, then revealed her intention to disguise herself. "Magic is forbidden there, so I'll have to pass as a warrior." The transformation took place in the armory. Althea donned light armor, each piece sliding onto her skin like a mother's caress. The armor contoured her body with precision that honored her silhouette, revealing not a warrior but the grace of a celestial dancer from Stellarae.

Iris, with a knowing chuckle, teased her comrade with her sharp wit. "Even dressed as a warrior, you still shine like a mage, Althea. Your skin has the softness of silk and the glow of stars, which is quite unusual for fighters."

Althea, with a playful smile, gracefully accepted the compliment with a theatrical curtsy. "Then, I shall be the most formidable dancer from Stellarae, and my dance will be one of illusion and mystery." Assuming the role of a dancer would allow her to keep her magical jewels without raising suspicion.

Their steps quickly led them to the docks where they boarded a shuttle connecting Solara to Lunaris. As they moved away from the quay, the city of Solara seemed to fade into a veil of morning light, while Lunaris awaited silently, like a specter in the morning fog.

In Lunaris, the differences were striking. The sun, obscured by clouds of sand, gave the city a twilight atmosphere in broad daylight. The numerous inhabitants masking their faces against the sand added to the city's aura of mystery.

In the maze of Lunaris's streets, Althea gestured gracefully towards the strange runes etched into the stone walls. Their winding outlines seemed to dance a silent melody that spoke of ancient prohibitions and distrust. "Anti-magic runes," she stated, her voice vibrating with knowledge as deep as the roots of the Maridora mountains. "Ruby wasn't mistaken."

Iris, whose sharp eye never missed an opportunity for a teasing jab, observed Althea with a smile that was not without mischief. "And here is our starry dancer from Stellarae, whose only spell is the whirl of her steps. Beware of the hearts you might bewitch with such attire."

Althea, maintaining her composure, quickly retorted with a smile playing at the corner of her mouth, betraying her amusement. "And you, Iris, be careful that the desert wind doesn't blunt your usual sharpness." Their light exchanges, like a breeze, reflected the complicity binding these two adventurous souls.

In the winding alleys of Lunaris, Iris and Althea moved cautiously, the air heavy with mysteries and unfathomable secrets. The facades of the houses, eroded by the desert winds, stood like silent sentinels, witnesses to stories buried under the sands of time.

Determined to find a place to rest their minds and bodies, they opted for a discreet inn. A place where, sheltered from prying eyes, they could unravel the complex fabric of their new enigma.

The choice fell on "The Traveler's Haven," a modest establishment known for its discretion.

Althea, while signing the register, exchanged a meaningful look with Iris. "We need a plan," she whispered. "Lunaris is a labyrinth, and Valerius could be anywhere."

Iris nodded, eyeing the surroundings warily. "I doubt the locals will be inclined to help two strangers."

They took possession of a modest but comfortable room, a temporary haven in this enigmatic city. As the sun began to set, they prepared to explore the winding alleys and well-kept secrets of Lunaris, the city where shadows of the past threatened to reemerge at every corner.

Their investigation led them to traverse the bustling districts of Lunaris, where merchants' voices intertwined with the tinkling of jewelry. The markets overflowed with riches, from fabrics in the colors of dawn to spices with scents from afar, each stall concealing its own shadows.

In a quieter alleyway, their attention was captured by unusual markings on the walls: anti-magic runes. "More runes," Althea observed, her gaze sharp.

Blending into the crowd, they subtly probed the neighborhood's memories, searching for traces of a lost mage. Eventually, a wrinkled merchant, her face a map of old age, provided them with a clue. Althea, cunningly, had mentioned her master's preference for fruits from the south. "A man, looking like a mage, did indeed purchase three baskets of my best harvest recently," confirmed the old vendor in a voice as cracked as leather. "A small purchase from you, and I can show you where I delivered them."

With discreet malice, the old woman offered to lead them to the destination. Iris's eyes gleamed fiercely, a sign of a trail finally found. "We'll follow you," she declared, her hand ever ready to wield her hidden dagger.

The merchant led them through a maze of alleys, each turn taking them deeper into a labyrinth of stone and mysteries. The walls seemed to whisper ancient stories, and their footsteps echoed heavily with anticipation on the cobblestones worn by ages.

As night fell, Iris and Althea found themselves back at the inn, their minds buzzing with information and theories. The old woman had led them to a place which, according to her, was the last known residence of Valerius in Lunaris. But it was now empty, hastily abandoned.

"We're on the right track," said Althea, scrutinizing an old grimoire she had found in Valerius's hideout.

"But each answer brings new questions."

Iris, despite the fatigue weighing on her shoulders, nodded with determination. "Tomorrow, we resume the hunt. We will find Valerius, no matter how long it takes." Her quest had started as a personal desire for answers, but now it carried the weight of Althea's and Diane's hopes. Her life had been a series of missions dictated by others, an existence devoted to blind obedience. Today, she was fighting for a purpose she had chosen, a path where her will, long confiscated, was finally asserting itself with strength.

In the silence of their room, the two women prepared to rest, aware that the coming days would test them like never before. Lunaris held its secrets tight, but they were determined to unravel them, no matter the cost.

* * *

Abyssal Beauty

In the dawning light of Lunaris, the city awoke to the sweltering heat rising from the burning sands of Naragath. The streets, still deserted, buzzed with the murmur of early merchants and guards changing shifts. The amber light of the rising sun lazily stretched between the tall towers and domes of the palaces, caressing the ochre stone of the city with a gentle embrace.

Althea, a mage of infinite intellect and unfathomable soul, had anticipated this moment with meticulous precision. In the quiet of their inn room, she presented Iris with fine, elegant diadems, woven with subtle magic and protective arcana. "Remember, these jewels are not just adornments," she reminded, "They're not just a beacon in the night, they are also the fortress that will preserve our free will against the assaults of deceptive enchantments." Grasping the jewel, Iris couldn't prevent her mind from wandering back to the oppressive memory of the burning marsh, where even the air seemed a poison for the mind.

With a magician's care, Althea unveiled from her bag a series of ethereal crystals. "These stones are much more than simple gems," she began, holding one of the sparkling crystals between her fingers. "If fractured, they release a veil of delicate mist, a powder capable of dispelling illusions and revealing the hidden truth behind spells."

As they prepared to venture near Cassandra's palace, this mysterious sovereign whose charm seemed to extend far beyond the borders of her realm, Althea, in the guise of a Stellarae dancer, and Iris, the hardened assassin, transformed into pilgrims of grace and enigma, ready to face the mirages of temptation.

Approaching the palace, they were suddenly captivated by the spectacle of a royal procession. Cassandra, like a vision from the pages of an ancient tale, paraded through her crowd, a procession of light and darkness dancing around her. Her beauty was undeniable, a hypnotic mix of power and grace, threat and promise. Iris, through the mist of the diadems, sensed the magnetic fascination she exerted. "She's definitely from another world," she thought, more an intuition than a certainty, observing Cassandra's enchanting aura.

The Empress of Desires' attire was a visual symphony of majesty and seduction. Like a creature born of the night and the deepest dreams, she wore a dress that embodied the essence of elegance and mystery. The garment flowed around her like a river of ink under the moon, a dark fabric playing between revealing and eclipsing the lines of her body, a living sculpture shaped by divine whims.

The form-fitting and exquisite bodice was embroidered with gold and purple threads, drawing complex arabesques that seemed to whisper tales of ancient spells and ardent passions. The precious stones adorning her plunging neckline sparkled like captive stars, jewels plucked from the firmament to underline her unmatched beauty.

Her gloves, extending to her elbows, were of a deep black, lending her arms an elegance that defied the simplicity of their hue. Their texture seemed to absorb the surrounding light, only to return it in a discreet shimmer, evoking the iridescence of a distant Celestial River.

The fabric of her dress, in its graceful flow, flared into a cascade of material that danced with every movement, the hem brushing the ground with the dignity and grace of a sovereign from a bygone era. The necklace, an opulent gathering of luminous gems, and the gold embroideries snaking through the dark velvet, spoke of her unparalleled status, of an unquestioned authority that needed no diadem to assert her reign. Every move in this dress was an act of domination and grace, a perfect balance between elegance and audacity.

Her attire was not just an aesthetic choice; it was a declaration, a symbol of power that transcended magic or brute force, resting entirely on the undeniable presence of the one who wore it. In this outfit, Cassandra was the living embodiment of temptation and power, an earthly deity whose mere presence could bend the firmest wills and ignite the coldest hearts. She was the eternal muse, the epitome of seduction, carrying within her the promise of a lasting empire built not on lands or seas, but on the desires and dreams of all those who crossed her bewitching path.

Her jet-black hair cascaded voluptuously over her shoulders, framing a face with delicate, almost unreal features, yet marked by fierce determination. Her eyes, two celestial jewels of deep blue, reminiscent of the tranquil waters of a forgotten lagoon, shone with an inner light, as if sparks of ancient truth were trapped within. Their brilliance was that of an infinite sky, a vast azure expanse dotted with silvery reflections, mirroring the secrets of the abyssal depths.

Iris couldn't tear her gaze away from the sovereign. Cassandra embodied a beauty from another world, a perfection that transcended reality, flirting with the surreal. There she stood, bathed in the day's final rays, a captivating creature whose charisma seemed to weave a direct connection with the souls of those who beheld her. The Queen of Lunaris was a living painting, a masterpiece of sensuality and power, where every curve, every look, every gesture was imbued with magic as alluring as it was dangerous. Cassandra was the very essence of temptation, a presence that defied morality and reason. Her gait was a caress to the eyes, each movement a call to desire, each smile a deadly snare.

"I am Cassandra," she seemed to say through her silence, "a vision of splendor and dominion, mastering hearts and wills with the finesse of an enchanting melody. My reign is that of duality, a harmony between light and darkness, the sacred and the profane."

Feeling herself slipping, Iris murmured, "She is otherworldly," her voice dry with palpable fascination. Althea, by her side, remained stoic, her eyes fixed on the jewels adorning the queen, perceiving beyond their shine, the quiver of magic hidden within.

The crowd, spellbound, formed a living tide swaying to the rhythm of her steps. Each gesture, each smile of Cassandra was a wave that rippled through hearts, igniting them with wild passion or soothing them with whispers of peace. Iris felt the brush of this power, a wave that defied reason, a temptation whispering in the soul's ear songs of desire and power.

Deep down, Iris knew they were facing the purest embodiment of duality: a creature of sublime beauty, capable of elevating spirits or plunging them into the abyss of perdition. In Cassandra's gaze, one could read the open book of creation and destruction, each page a tale of seduction, each word a spell that could lead them to their doom or salvation.

In the turmoil of the royal procession, time seemed to stand still as Cassandra's impenetrable and abyssal gaze met Iris's. A chilling shiver ran through the assassin, her innermost thoughts exposed, her will shaken. It was a look that probed the soul, stripped the mind with surgical precision, an intrusion as terrifying as it was fascinating. Iris felt dispossessed, a veil torn away to reveal a vulnerability she had never allowed herself to acknowledge. This was the alienating power of a succubus. Without the diadem, she would have been reduced to a mere pawn, stripped of her essence.

When Cassandra's eyes met Althea's, an inaudible silence filled the space between them. Where Iris had been an easy target, Althea presented a challenge, a mystery to be deciphered. The succubus's face betrayed a hint of interest, an imperceptible smile flitting across Cassandra's lips. It was the trace of a smile that betrayed neither triumph nor defeat, but the pleasure of a player in the face of an unexpected move, the silent acknowledgment of a mind that would not be so easily unraveled. Althea did not flinch, challenging the abyss with a gaze as unfathomable as that of her opponent. In her eyes shone an indomitable light, a reflection of her own depth and complexity that resonated with Cassandra's darkness. The abyss gazing into the abyss.

It was a silent confrontation, but one heavily laden with unspoken intentions and the prospect of future clashes. Iris, defeated by the succubus's gaze, appeared broken. Althea suggested they retreat to safety. Already, her strategic mind was weaving the beginnings of a confrontation that would become a war of shadows and lights, a dance with the devil where only the most cunning could claim triumph.

As the procession moved away, leaving behind a trail of unanswered questions, Iris and Althea returned to the inn. Back in the solitude of their inn room, Iris collapsed onto the bed, her armor of confidence chipped by the ordeal she had just endured. The thick walls of the room seemed to smother the city's sounds, leaving only silence to accompany her troubled thoughts.

She remained there, motionless, her gaze fixed on the void. Then, like a dam bursting under the pressure of water held back for too long, tears began to flow, silent and relentless. Each drop was a confession, an admission of weakness that Iris had sworn never to show. Iris had never been trained for this kind of combat, against an opponent of this nature. Her strength, dexterity, and speed, though formidable, proved superfluous... She felt powerless. For the first time, the Black Rose wept, her tears becoming dewdrops on the petals of a flower that had resisted the storms for too long.

Althea, observing this scene of rare vulnerability, approached softly. She said nothing, choosing instead to sit next to Iris, offering her silent presence as an anchor in the emotional storm. Words were unnecessary; in this moment of shared fragility, support was found in the simple act of being there, a witness to each other's pain and strength.

Iris's tears were a symbol of an inner struggle, the battle of a warrior against her own demons. In the reflection of these tears, one could see the transformation of a hardened assassin, deprived of childhood, into a mere human facing her deepest fears, discovering her own humanity.

Iris had not been prepared for this kind of battle, this kind of adversary. Her strength, dexterity, and speed were superfluous... She was powerless.

The hours stretched on, and the shadow of the night enveloped everything. Without a word, Althea lay down next to Iris, in a simple but powerful gesture of unity and protection. Their breathing synchronized, and in the darkness, their silhouettes seemed less alone. The warrior and the mage, each fighting their own battles, found a moment of peace.

Iris, exhausted by the emotions of the day, felt the weight of her eyelids become insurmountable.

Beside her, Althea kept watch, a guardian against the shadows of the night. Finally, even Althea succumbed to the need for rest, confident in the security of their shared bond.

And so, in the tranquility of the night, they found sleep, one beside the other, two solitary souls united by a common path, their breaths mingling to form a single whisper in the silence.

❋ ❋ ❋

The Mirror Of The Soul

The first lights of dawn caressed their faces, gently rousing them from the remnants of an endless nightmare.
In the complex fabric of Lunaris, a trap was forming, invisible to the eye but evident to the young mage. Althea, with an impassive face and a gravity not customary to her, took time to gaze at Iris with uncommon intensity. "The beauty of Cassandra is a mirage, a gateway to an abyss that lurks for us all," she begins, her voice as soft as a distant melody. "She is the reflection of our most unspoken desires, an echo from the abysses of our own being."

Iris, attentive, allows her gaze to darken at the

thought of this upcoming confrontation. "This halo of beauty makes us vulnerable. It adorns the appearance with non-existent virtues, weaving a veil of perfection around the imperfect. What we see in Cassandra is an illusion shaped by our own mind, our own narcissism that draws us towards what we would like to be or possess."

Althea leaned forward, her hands joining as if to imprison a secret between their intertwined fingers. "It's a fight against the mirror, Iris. A battle where every reflection is a skirmish, every image a war against our buried desires. To borrow the words of a venerable sage, Nithz of Stellarae, 'if you gaze long into an abyss, the abyss also gazes into you'. Cassandra, she is that abyss. She sees us, she sees what we truly are, our vices and virtues."

"And that's why if we must face her, we must be armed not with blades or spells, but with self-knowledge. The strength to resist the call of what we secretly covet." Althea stood up, her eyes scanning the urban landscape of the city, each silhouette, each shadow a reminder of the struggle to come.

"We will oppose a creature that has probed the abysses of the human soul, who knows our weaknesses, our cardinal sins. It might be the most dangerous power of all, Iris. The one that confronts us not with an external enemy, but with the one that resides within us, lurking in the shadow of our own reflection."

Iris, with clenched fists, nodded in agreement. She now understood the nature of the struggle, a confrontation where victory is not measured by the strength of weapons, but by the resilience of the spirit. "Then we shall be warriors of the spirit, Althea. We will fight against the reflection until the true face is revealed, in all its light or darkness."

"Yes, Iris, the time for confrontation has come," responded Althea.

In a silence filled with mutual understanding, they descended for breakfast to gather the strength needed to face the new day.

CHAPTER 13: CONFRONTATION

Gather!

In the warm morning air, they descended for a breakfast that resembled more a ritual preceding battle. To their great surprise and profound emotion, they discovered Ruby and their travel companions already seated at the table: Diane, Celestia, Mirela, and Ukrolm. The contrast between the joy of reunion and the burden of recent events was striking.

The embraces exchanged within the group vibrated with a unique energy, and sincere smiles lit up every face in the room. Anecdotes from their respective journeys flew, tinged with humor and bravery, bringing a much-needed moment of lightness. However, Iris and Althea remained cautious about their recent encounter with Cassandra, choosing not to burden their companions with alarming details.

Diane, with her innate grace, scrutinized Iris and Althea, seeking clues about their findings in Lunaris. Her concern was palpable, shared by Celestia, whose radiant face was shadowed under the weight of her responsibilities.

Ukrolm, imposing and solemn, listened attentively, while Mirela brought a calm and composed presence, filling the room with serenity.

What had started as a morning meal quickly turned into a strategic council. Sketches of plans emerged on scattered pieces of paper, maps of the city were spread out and meticulously annotated. Their objective was defined with stark clarity: they needed to confront Cassandra to unveil the truths hidden behind her reign in Lunaris.

Ruby, the mischievous one, offered her skills to gather additional information. Her knowledge of Lunaris's alleys could prove decisive in their quest for truth.

A mixed feeling of determination and apprehension animated the group. The upcoming adversary was of an incomprehensible nature, both enchanting and formidable.

It was Althea who spoke up, instilling confidence and measured thought in her words. "Each of us has a crucial role to play. Every action, every choice matters. It's together that we will make a difference."

Iris, usually so composed, echoed Althea with an intensity that transformed her. "Strength lies in our unity. Our diversity of skills and knowledge is our greatest asset. By combining our abilities, we will find a way to overthrow Cassandra."

A collective nod sealed their union. They were aware that the coming hours would be crucial, but in this new dawn, a feeling of unwavering preparedness inhabited them. Together, they were ready to face the challenges, whatever the cost.

Althea, with a confidence that betrayed her meticulous preparation, stood up to reveal the plan. "We are going to confront the succubus. I have observed her personal guard. If we use crystal powder, we could temporarily free them from the enchantment, or at least disorient them enough to reach Cassandra."

Ruby, with a sparkle of irony in her eye, interjected, "And how are you going to use it without magic? Are you going to offer her a dance?" Laughter echoed around the table, as Althea blushed slightly, her authority as a leader temporarily shaken by her unusual attire.

Regaining her seriousness, Althea explained, "The magic concerns Celestia and me. Most anti-magic runes do not affect the divine magic of paladins. And I have brought some potions, crystals, and artifacts to help us."

Ruby, curious, asked, "Your crystal powder, can it neutralize the enchantment if applied directly to the succubus?"

Althea nodded. "That's a possibility. But we would need to get close enough."

Diane then suggested: "I could use an arrow to scatter the powder on her from a distance."

Impressed, Althea continued, "Ukrolm, Celestia, you will be in charge of clearing a path for us. Iris, I know you're worried, but Celestia, as a high-ranking paladin, is immune to mental domination. As for Ukrolm, it's a risk we must take. Mirela's blessing spells will help us resist psychic magic. Each of you will carry a crystal, in case of danger, break it."

Then, she turned to Ruby: "Your mission will be to find Valerius and free him. He could be a significant ally."

The looks they exchanged were filled with determination. They were ready to plunge into battle, united in their resolution to defeat Cassandra and save Valerius.

❊ ❊ ❊

The Battle In The Throne Room

The progression through the alleys of Lunaris

was carried out with a silent, almost ritualistic determination. Iris and Althea, as scouts, set a brisk pace, closely followed by the impassive procession of Ukrolm, Celestia, Mirela, and Diane. Ruby, an agile and discreet specter, slipped between the shadows, ever watchful.

Their advance, radiating a fervent resolve, blended into the fabric of legends. Cloaked in inconspicuous capes that masked their armors, they moved in a spectral phalanx, a ghostly procession emerging from the darkness to claim justice.

At the outskirts of the palace, they deceived the first guards with an almost theatrical ruse, their passage remaining unchallenged. But as they penetrated the inner courtyards, confrontation became inevitable. Celestia and Ukrolm, instruments of celestial and terrestrial fury, carved a path through their adversaries with a rigor that bordered on grace. Mirela, weaver of blessings, emboldened her comrades with a touch of the divine. Celestia, resplendent in her role as a bulwark, captured the wrath of the assailants, while Ukrolm, unshakable, dismantled their ranks with the regularity of a warrior metronome.

Diane, for her part, orchestrated a deadly ballet with her bow, each arrow released finding its target with a precision that bordered on artistry. Her talent rivaled the legendary skill of the archers of the ancient woods, astonishing her companions with her mastery. With a mischievous wink, she quipped, "A defenseless princess, you say?" Her witty remark added a welcome lightness in the midst of battle.

Althea, aware that time was of the essence with the imminent arrival of enemy reinforcements, urged the group to advance into the palace. Inside, she assigned Ukrolm and Celestia the crucial task of securing the entrance, thus forming an impenetrable bulwark against any outside assault. Meanwhile, the rest of the team, bolstered by Mirela, rushed towards the palace's central hall.

Emerging from the shadows, Ruby brought critical information: Valerius was nowhere to be found in the east wing. "I'll continue my search," she declared, before vanishing into the darkness as suddenly as she had appeared.

The group reached the massive doors of the throne room unimpeded. The striking contrast between the calm of the hall and the chaos of the battles outside hung heavy in the air. In front of the imposing doors, they gathered, mentally and physically preparing for the ultimate confrontation. This showdown would determine not just the future of Lunaris, but their own as well.

Diane, with palpable concern in her voice, alerted the group. "This quiet is too suspicious. Be ready for a less than warm welcome." Beside her, Iris, her hand tightly clenched around her protective crystal, nodded gravely. "Let's act with the swiftness and precision of lightning," she retorted, a glint of determination in her eyes.

Mirela, the wise priestess, wove shielding spells around the group, enveloping them in an invisible yet resolutely tangible protective aura. The decisive moment had arrived. With a determined gesture, Iris pushed open the monumental doors of the throne room.

The interior was charged with an oppressive atmosphere, a blend of palpable power and threats. Cassandra, the Empress of Desires, sat on her throne with an artificially displayed weariness, her eyes concealing calculated malice. To her left, Valerius, the missing archmage, had a vacant, almost ghostly look. To her right stood an intimidating black knight and a predatory-looking ranger.

The group faced this menacing assembly, each member aware of the magnitude of the challenge awaiting them.

Cassandra greeted them with a smooth, sarcastic voice. "You took your time." Her presence filled the room, each word a venom wrapped in honey.

Without hesitation, Iris charged, an arrow of fury

and determination, straight towards the heart of the enemy. But her assault met an invisible magical barrier, an impenetrable wall of force, seemingly maintained by Valerius himself. Diane, in a reflexive gesture, fired three arrows that shattered against this same defense.

Althea, the strategic mind of the group, immediately grasped the urgency. "We must break this barrier!" Her hands performed a rapid dance, weaving a spell to dissipate the magical protection. But as their obstacle evaporated, the battle plunged into a whirlwind of chaos.

The black knight lunged at Diane with impressive speed for an armored warrior, while the ranger rushed towards Mirela, aiming to neutralize the vital support of the group. Althea, her heart pounding furiously, analyzed the situation with lightning speed but felt overwhelmed by the rapid turn of events.

In a desperate move, Iris threw a crystal towards Valerius, shouting a warning to Diane, and rushed to protect Mirela from the ranger. Diane, choosing a sacrificial act, aimed at the mage rather than dodging the impending attack. The arrow, guided by a determined spirit, found its target, turning the crystal to dust and lodging in Valerius's arm. Liberated and wounded, he wavered and fell. Time seemed suspended, each gesture eternally marking the course of their destiny.

Celestia, like a goddess of war, burst into the fray. "This one is mine!" she roared, confronting the black knight with divine fury, saving Diane from a fatal fate.

Althea, paralyzed by the intensity of the battle, watched her companions fight with bravery. Iris, though gravely wounded in the intervention, faced the ranger with unwavering courage. Celestia, in a dance of iron and fire, battled the black knight.

Althea realized too late that Cassandra was rising from her throne, her eyes locking onto Diane's. In a flash of clarity, Althea hurled crystals at the succubus, cutting her skin. "Pathetic," Cassandra spat with disdain.

"You won't have my mind," retorted Althea, a glint of defiance in her eyes.

Cassandra, revealing her demonic form with dark wings unfurled, responded with a voice that was both a caress and a blade, "We are not so different, you and I, witch..."

Althea, consumed by a blazing fury, hurled a ball of energy, sparkling with crystalline glimmers, striking Cassandra squarely and propelling her against the wall. Her attacks, merging shades of purple and violet, erupted with scorching intensity. "I am nothing like you, demon!" she cried out, each burst of magic hitting its target with relentless force, revealing the depth of her determination and the power of her magic.

The battle reached its climax, with blows landing with devastating force. Celestia conquered the black knight, while Iris, despite her injuries, vanquished the ranger. But this victory came at a price: Althea collapsed, exhausted and bruised. Cassandra, inscrutable, escaped through a mysterious portal, leaving behind words that echoed like a dark prophecy: "What I learned today is worth many defeats."

Silence fell upon the throne room, filled with the heaviness of sacrifices made and bitter victories. The battle was over, but the war, the war still continued in the hearts of those who remained standing.

Althea, whose eyes still sparkled with the last glimmer of her power, collapsed, defeated by fatigue and the subsiding intensity of adrenaline. The throne room, once a symbol of terror and intrigue, now transformed into the scene of a poignant triumph, albeit tinged with pain. Each member of the team had played a decisive role in the outcome of this conflict, showcasing extraordinary courage, strength, and determination.

Iris, approaching Althea, her face marked by the

stigmas of battle, whispered: "We have succeeded." But the price of their victory was evident in her tired eyes, revealing the depths of their inner struggle. The Black Rose had faced its demons and had held firm.

Diane, shaking her head to free herself from Cassandra's mental grasp, rushed to Mirela, now unconscious on the ground. "Stay with us," she pleaded, a tear of despair and hope welling in the corner of her eye.

Celestia, having vanquished the black knight, turned to her companions, her golden armor dulled by dust and blood. "And now?" she inquired, her gaze settling on Althea, now lifeless.

Iris, her own wounds seemingly healing as if by magic, answered with a voice charged with resolution. "Go find news of Ukrolm. We need him to transport the wounded!" Her voice, firm despite the fatigue, carried a clear command and unwavering determination.

CHAPTER 14:
EPILOGUE

After The Storm

When Althea regained consciousness, she was greeted by the familiar faces of Mirela, Iris, and Valerius, a feeling of relief and joy overwhelming her. Sitting up gently, she asked in a still weak voice, "Diane?"

Valerius, reassuringly, replied, "She's at the palace. She's managing the transition of power with the help of Ruby, who brings her knowledge of the city. Celestia is ensuring her protection." He paused, adding in a grave tone, "Cassandra's ravages are deep, some even invisible. I have requested the aid of priests and mages to support Diane in this task."

Worried, Althea then asked, "And Ukrolm?"

Iris, with a reassuring smile, assured her. "He's resting. We found him exhausted, but his wounds are healing quickly. He's resilient, our colossus."

Althea, thinking of Iris, inquired, "And you, Iris? You were gravely injured..."

Iris, with a hint of mystery in her voice, confided, "It's strange. The moment you defeated the succubus, my wounds began to heal. Perhaps it's due to Mirela's magic?"

Althea, with a penetrating gaze, revealed, "No, it's your magic, Iris. The diadem you wore in the marsh allowed me to discover that you have a potential in light magic. Your injuries awakened what I now call the 'Arcanes of the Black Rose', the Light Assassin."

Valerius, rising, suggested, "Now that you're recovered, let's join the banquet hall of the palace. A feast is planned in our honor."

Upon arriving at the banquet, everyone was dazzled by the splendor of Diane. Dressed in her royal attire, she radiated a stunning beauty, her golden hair falling in perfect waves, reflecting light as if strands of sunlight were woven through her curls. She evoked the image of a benevolent and majestic queen, her luminous presence contrasting with the darkness of Cassandra, thus embodying the other facet of beauty - one that liberates and uplifts the spirit.

Around the lavishly adorned tables, the hall resonated with an atmosphere both solemn and light. The hosts shared their recent epics, their voices mixing bursts of laughter with memories of dangers overcome, all while savoring the exquisite dishes prepared for the celebration. Mirela, a discreet but attentive presence, was not yet healed from her injuries. Yet, she lent a benevolent ear to each tale, her face lighting up with a smile imbued with sweetness and resilience.

Iris, a battle companion sitting close to Althea, silently contemplated Diane's transformation. The princess, once mystifying and distant, now stood before them as a symbol of hope and rebirth. Her natural grace, her aura of nobility, commanded everyone's admiration. Even Althea, known for her reserve, found herself moved by the serene majesty emanating from Diane, an aura of greatness that touched the hearts of those who beheld her.

The evening unfolded under the signs of camaraderie and renewed hope. Every laugh, every exchange, strengthened the bonds formed during their journey. The joy of victory was tempered by the awareness of past trials and future challenges.

As the night progressed, Valerius took the floor. His voice, deep and comforting, captivated the audience. "Tonight, we celebrate not only a victory but also courage, tenacity, and unity. Our fight against the forces of darkness is far from over, but together, we have proven that light can triumph."

The feast concluded with a solemn toast to the future. Each member of the group, aware of the journey behind them and the battles ahead, felt invigorated by the spirit of fraternity and shared determination. The night ended on a note of hope, each knowing that, despite uncertainties, they were now bound by a common destiny and a cause greater than themselves.

❊ ❊ ❊

The Meanders Of Truth

The following day was devoted to revelations and new riddles.

When Iris revealed to Valerius the puzzling words of the priestess of Valoria, a shadow of concern crossed his face. The implications of this revelation – Iris as a possible second daughter of Eliora, Mirela's sister – brought a flood of emotions and memories. A heavy silence settled in, as Valerius, overwhelmed by the past, searched for his words with caution.

"It is essential that I verify your origins before revealing what I know," said Valerius, his voice betraying a hesitation mixed with hope. "Such a consequential assertion cannot be made lightly. It could forever change the course of your life, as well as that of others…"

Rising, Valerius approached Iris. His gaze, intense and scrutinizing, seemed to search Iris's features for the shadow of Eliora. "Your resemblance to her is striking. She was a precious friend, and if you are her daughter... it awakens in me a wave of emotions I thought had calmed."

A contemplative silence followed, with Valerius appearing to converse with his thoughts. "I must confirm this truth with tangible evidence and magical verifications," he continued, "Can you recall exactly what the priestess said at Valoria? Every word, every nuance could be the key."

Iris, grasping the importance of her memories, faithfully shared the priestess's words, while Valerius, absorbed, weighed the hidden meaning behind each of them.

"If this is confirmed, you could be the lost daughter of Eliora, Mirela's sister. However, I refuse to lull you with illusions or reopen old wounds without formal proof. Especially since Mirela knows nothing of her own origins." Valerius placed a benevolent hand on Iris's shoulder, his look filled with empathetic seriousness. "I promise to uncover the truth. You have the right to know your real story."

Overwhelmed by the implications of these revelations, Iris silently nodded, finding some comfort in Valerius's determination. The idea of a rediscovered family reignited a flame of hope in her, tinged with natural apprehension.

Valerius, returning to the rest of the group, shared his assumptions. "The presence of the black knight alongside Cassandra clearly indicates that Sarthax is involved. And this inevitably points to the necromancer's influence in these events."

He paused, weighing each word. "It is essential to analyze the implications of this alliance. Cassandra would not act as an ally of Sarthax without finding her own benefit. There is certainly more to uncover about their mutual designs."

"Which means," he continued with measured gravity, "that the fall of Cassandra is just one closed chapter. The necromancer, and Sarthax in particular, remain imminent threats. Our vigilance must not wane; preparation is key to facing what lies ahead."

The echo of his words spread among the assembly, reinforcing the collective awareness of the gravity and complexity of the situation. The defeat of Cassandra was but one step, a prelude to a far larger conflict, pitting the companions against enemies of formidable power and cunning.

It was then that Althea intervened, her voice filled with unwavering determination: "Whatever path lies ahead of us, the next step in our quest is clear. We must free the Queen of Valoria from a malevolent grip and thwart the plots of the necromancer and his destructive schemes."

Althea's assurance, crystallized in the attentive silence of her allies, rang out like a call to arms, not for war, but for the preservation of the world's balance. "The necromancer's actions have shaken the very foundations of our existence. His quest for power threatens the harmony that keeps our realms in peace."

She swept her gaze across the assembly, an unyielding glimmer shining in her eyes. "What we have achieved, the union of our forces against Cassandra, is the dazzling proof of our potential. It is now imperative to channel our collective power to defend our world and foil the plots of the necromancer."

Her speech, imbued with a contagious assurance, infused the group with new vigor. "Our path will not be easy, that much is certain. But I am convinced that together, nothing can impede our march towards victory." Althea's words, charged with unshakable confidence, imprinted themselves in the minds of all, united by a common cause — that of justice and the preservation of peace.

❋ ❋ ❋

The Ghosts Of The Past

On the peaceful shores of Lake Blanc, the sacred enclosure of the Solis sanctuary bathed in an almost tangible tranquility. The high priestess, a figure of calm and comfort, gazed at the shimmering waters, a perfect mirror of the azure sky above. The trees lining the lake stood still, as if in prayer, and the songs of birds wove a melody that seemed to celebrate the harmony of nature.

She walked slowly onto the forecourt, her bare feet brushing the sacred ground with respect, each step a meditation, each breath a silent thanksgiving to life. The air was imbued with the essence of wildflowers and the subtle aroma of the herbs from the priestesses' garden, a sanctuary within the sanctuary where time seemed suspended.

In this enclave of serenity, the arrival of the messenger falcon was almost surreal. The bird, seen by some as a manifestation of divine will, sliced through the serene sky with a grace that contrasted the gravity of the news it carried. It landed with a delicacy that betrayed the urgency of its flight.

With measured gestures, the priestess unrolled the message, her eyes quickly scanning the lines written by a familiar hand. The content of the message was brief, but laden with meaning:

*"Chaos magic.
We need to talk.*

Valerius."

* * *

To be continued...

THE CHRONICLES OF ELYSORIUM

"The Chronicles of Elysorium" is an epic series that transports you to the heart of an enchanted world where magic and myths intertwine in a breathtaking temporal tapestry. From the bewitching jungles of Stellarae to the snowy peaks of Frostend, from resplendent cities to verdant realms, each place is a character in its own right. The protagonists, from the powerful mage to the fearless warrior, from the heroic paladin to the dark assassin, enrich this living tapestry with intrigue and ancient wisdom. Follow the echoes of magic and the whispers of gods in an adventure where each end marks a new epic beginning.

The Chronicles Of Elysorium 2 - Chaos Theory

Dive into the heart of the arcane in this captivating second volume. Between science and sorcery, discover the origins of chaos magic and the mysteries of entropy threatening the balance of

Elysorium. Follow Althea in her quest for truth and find out if Iris can escape the shadows of her past. [Forthcoming]

The Chronicles Of Elysorium 3 - Fire And Lightning

In this dazzling third installment, follow the steps of Iridia Skyfury and Hestia Carmina, two mages whose legendary powers shape the destiny of Elysorium. When celestial fire meets divine lightning, an unlikely alliance forms to confront a threat that could engulf their world in the flames of chaos. [Forthcoming]

The Chronicles Of Elysorium 4 - Sands Of Oblivion

Enter the desert of Tokamak, where the sands of oblivion whisper legends erased by time. Discover the mysteries buried under the relentless dunes, where memories blend with mirages. [Forthcoming]

Made in the USA
Las Vegas, NV
27 January 2024